CHUWA
THE RAT-PEOPLE
OF LAHORE

BOOK ONE OF
THE CHUWA COVENANT

Also by Brian Craddock

Short Fiction
The Red Heart
The Angel of Isisford
Plato's Cave
The Black Shuck
The Blue Frog Falls
The Cemetery Children
Punk's Not Dead
Wisdom and Madness
Atishfishan
Mumbles Pier

Novels
Eucalyptus Goth

Collected Works
The Dalziel Files

Essays
Defining the Body Horror Concept within
Clive Barker's *Nightbreed* (The Body Horror Book)

CHUWA

THE RAT-PEOPLE OF LAHORE

BRIAN CRADDOCK

BROKEN
PUPPET

CHUWA: The Rat-People of Lahore

Book One in The Chuwa Covenant series

Text Copyright © 2019 Brian Craddock
Cover Copyright © 2019 Brian Craddock

FOR BROKEN PUPPET BOOKS

www.brokenpuppetbooks.com

ISBN-13: 978-0-6481128-2-2
Printed in Australia

MAP OF LAHORE

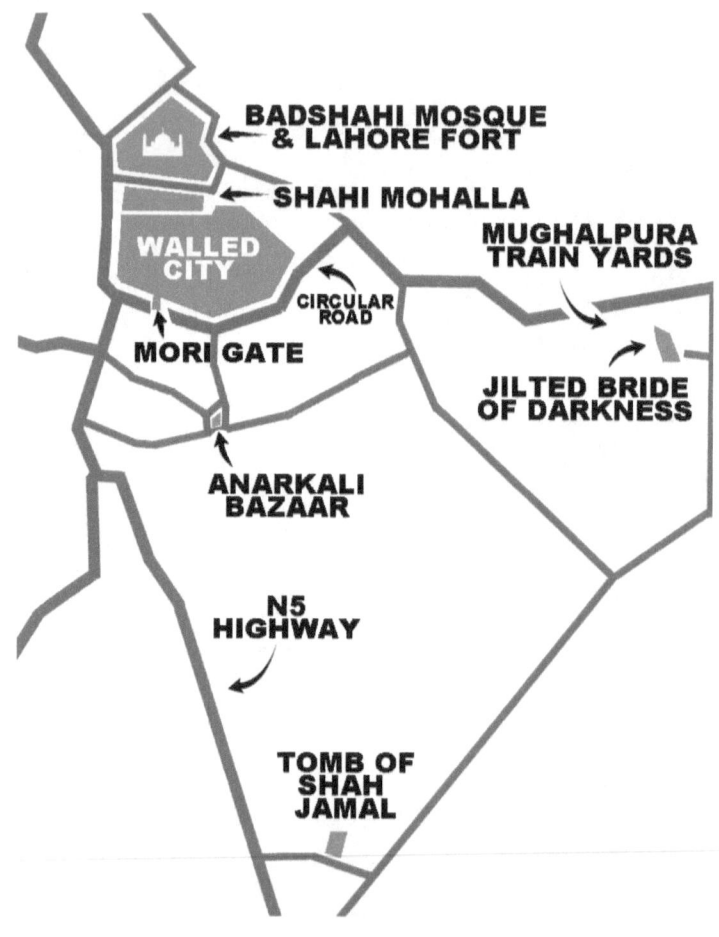

Glossary

Aacha	Right. Okay. I understand
Abbu	Father
Ammi	Mother
Ammi-ji	Mother dearest
Azhan	The Muslim call to prayer
Baaga	A militant style of Punjabi dance
Baba	An honorific, meaning "wise old man" or "sir"
Badmash	Mafia
Baji-ji	Older sister
Bara	Big
Bas	Enough/Stop
Beedi	A thin cigarette of betel nut, herbs, and spices, all wrapped in a tendu (East Indian ebony) leaf
Bhai	Brother – used for non-relations
Bhari-jaga	A "heavy" place; haunted location.
Biriyani	A popular mixed rice dish in Pakistan and India.
Chaal	Movements of traditional Punjabi dance
Chelo	Let's go

Dadi	Grandmother, on father's side
Dhol	Drum
Dholi	Person who plays the *dhol*
Djinn	Genies, spirits, or demons Islamic mythology and theology
Dulhan	bride
Dupatta	Head scarf, or shawl
Goonda	Gangster or mafia member
Goree	White/foreign lady
Gulab jamun	A syrupy, milk-solid-based sweet from the Indian subcontinent, popular in Pakistan
Hai'na	An expression of inquiry or slight surprise. Equivalent of English "eh".
Harrapan	Relating to the ancient Bronze-Age city of Harappa, part of the Indus Valley Civilisation in present-day Pakistan.
Haveli	A traditional townhouse, usually with historical and architectural significance
Jaldi	Quick/hurry
Jannu	Dear – term of endearment
-ji	Suffix meaning dearest
Kakaul	A hat made from Qaraqul wool, a breed of sheep. It originates from Afghanistan
Lathi	A bamboo rod, used for beating

Masjid	Mosque
Mehndi	Henna markings, particularly for weddings
Meribani	Thank-you
Najumi	Fortune-teller
Pakol	A soft round-topped woollen hat, especially worn in Northern Pakistan
Paow	Goat feet stew
Papa-ji	Father dearest – mix of English and Urdu
Pota	Son's son (grandson)
Saab	Punjabi honorary when addressing a boss, used after their name
Shabash	Well done! Congratulations!
Shab-bakhair	Good-night
Shalwar-Kameez	The traditional apparel in the Punjab region: *shalwar* (baggy trousers) and *kameez* (long tunic), usually paired with a *dupatta* (head scarf).
Sherwani	Long garment worn by groom
Tandoor	Clay oven for cooking bread or meat
Walima	The fifth day of the Islamic wedding ceremony
Wallah	A suffix meaning "one in charge" (eg: a rickshaw driver is a rickshaw-wallah)

"Nau sau chuhe khake billi haj ko
chali."

"After eating nine-hundred rats, the cat
goes on pilgrimage."

– ancient Indian proverb

PROLOGUE

THEN

Through the shadowed streets two figures in robes passed, eager to be done with their errand before the call to first prayer. The streets were practically deserted at this time of morning, but come the *azhan* the desolation would be forsaken, and so, too, their cover. Time was of the essence.

At their feet flowed a shifting tide, undulating as it swept around corners, keeping pace with the robed errand-keepers. It squeaked and squabbled with its progress, this tide did, claw and tooth flashing from its dark currents. Only when it followed its masters across the road did the dull illumination of the street-light show the gnashing tide to be a river of rats, squabbling amongst themselves for prize place closest to the feet of the errand-keepers.

A homeless man sat up from his bedding of tarpaulin as the tide approached, beseeching the figures for alms, just a modest token of generosity with which he might purchase some flat-bread later in the day. He was summarily ignored, by the errand-keepers, at least; but of the rats that followed, not so. They swarmed toward the man before he had sense enough to flee, enveloping him and stifling any cry for help he might have been ready to beckon.

The errand-keepers didn't break their stride, confident the horde of rats would find their way through the maze of laneways once they'd finished with their meal.

Into the narrow lanes of the Walled City did the two figures proceed, winding their way through the impossible labyrinth swiftly and without need of a map.

Ansoor Makhdoom knelt before his family, huddled together on the floor beside the hearth, his spectacles white with the reflection of the fire. His wife had wrapped her arms around their son, Wasim, and their daughter-in-law Bilqees, who held a swathed bundle to her bosom. Despite the warmth of the hearth, the poor girl was so terrified she was shivering, so Ansoor fetched another blanket from the wardrobe, draping it over his daughter-in-law. She clutched at it with fingers like claws, the *mehndi* whorls darker than ever against her whitening knuckles, while the other hand held fast to the baby.

Ordinarily, the baby's head would have been shaved and a sheep sacrificed on the seventh day of its birth, as was the custom, but necessities dictated custom take a back-seat for once. Ansoor had received plenty of criticism from family and neighbours for the deviance from tradition, but these censures mattered not to Ansoor when it was his grandson's life on the line. Family and friends would eventually forgive him, he figured, though they'd likely not let him forget it. A small price to pay.

"Dearest, check the marks again," his wife, Malika, urged.

Ansoor nodded, inspecting the chalk sigils scrawled on the inside of the window shutters, and on the door. Taking a piece of chalk from his pocket, he traced over the looped configurations again for good measure, twisting the chalk in their centres for the dots. The gypsies had been adamant no part of the sigil be neglected.

"The tickets are with you?" Ansoor asked his son while he worked the chalk.

Wasim nodded, his face impassive.

"Don't worry, *abbu*," he said, patting his shirt pocket where he'd folded the aeroplane tickets for he, Bilqees, and their baby. "I'm sure everything will be okay. But you should come with us, you and moth–"

"No, enough of that," Ansoor said, turning from the door and crossing back to his family. "It is not us they want."

As if by a summons, there came a scratching at the door. Ansoor spun on his heel, eyes wide and fear in his guts. He dared not breathe, let alone speak. The scratching continued unabated, accompanied by a scraping sound, as of timber being carved by a whittling knife. The chalk sigils were bold, the lines thick and solid. He'd been promised they'd with-stand attack, that the ones who sought his family could not breach their power. He'd begun to suspect he'd been taken for a fool.

"*Abbu!*"

Wasim had forsaken the arms of his mother, and of his young wife, to stand beside his father, ready for a fight.

"Whatever happens, you must take Bilqees and get to the airport, son," Ansoor said, squeezing his son's shoulder, and noting with some concern the reluctance he saw in Wasim's eyes. "Promise me, son. You must promise me."

Wasim shook his head, struggling with the decision, but heard himself agree. His voice sounded far-away.

Ansoor turned to face the door again, in time to see it drop from its hinges. It slowly tipped forward, forcing father and son to leap back as it accelerated and crashed onto the rug at their feet. Dust flew up, obscuring their vision. Behind them, Bilqees shrieked.

Wiping his spectacles clean, Ansoor saw two figures beyond the doorway, obscured by hooded robes. Circling the door-jamb were a hundred rats, their beady black eyes staring impassively in at him. He glanced down at the door, noting the wood had been gnawed at, especially around the hinges. The rats had chewed the door free, and Ansoor's sigils hadn't been meant for natural creatures.

"Chuwa!" shouted Wasim, having wiped the dust free from his face and, spying the hooded figures beyond the doorway, had stepped before his father and pointed in accusation.

Ansoor grabbed his son and pulled him away, shoving him back toward the women.

"Protect them," he demanded.

The hooded figures – the chuwa – crossed the threshold, the talons of their toes clacking on the concrete floor. The rats followed, swarming down the doorjamb and leaping over one another as they skirted the room, closing in on the women huddled in the corner.

Wasim took up a *lathi*, a bamboo rod, and began beating the rats back.

"Stay the hell away from my family, you monsters!" shouted Ansoor.

He rushed the chuwa, fists raised, but was beaten to the floor with a backhand.

"*Abbu!*"

"Protect the baby," Ansoor ordered his son.

The chuwa stood before the cowering women, and extended a hand, palm-upturned. The skin was calloused, and deeply lined, and where there should have been nails, there protruded claws.

"The child, as owed," said one of the intruders, its voice like sandpaper.

Wasim threw himself at the chuwa, knocking one to the floor. The hood fell away to reveal a creature scarcely human: in place of a mouth and nose it sported a snout, and its long incisors looked lethal; dark marbles for eyes rolled in its sockets, and its entire face and skull were punched with coarse hair.

"The child is owed us," it repeated, clutching Wasim by his shirt-front and pulling him close. Its foetid breath made him ill, its incisors so close to Wasim's face he felt the enamel of its teeth brush his nose when the creature spoke. "Get in my way again, and you will most certainly die."

He was shoved away with such strength he found himself flung halfway across the room, landing on the fallen door. A sharp pain lanced up his side, making him gasp.

Bilqees was on her feet now, back pressed against the wall, holding tight to her precious bundle. From amongst the folds of cloth came a baby's squall.

"You cannot have my baby," she shrieked at the intruders.

The chuwa ignored her, advancing with claws outstretched.

"Jamallan!" called Wasim, from behind.

The chuwa turned to see a sigil rushing at them. Wasim slammed the door into the face of one of the creatures, stunning it briefly, thrilled to see it fall to its knees. The second creature backed away as Wasim wielded the door – or more correctly, the chalk sigil scrawled upon its surface. He forced the chuwa to back up slowly, its hands raised in supplication.

Hearing his wife demand the other chuwa stay away, Wasim's attention was diverted. Bilqees waved the fire stoker at her attacker, threatening to burn it.

The chuwa at Wasim's back grinned, bringing its hands together in a single clap. The rats in the room responded, charging across the floor toward Wasim, nipping at his feet and climbing his legs. He dropped the door in order to swat the vermin off his body, sending it crashing into the glass-front cabinet. Shards of glass rained down onto the rug, slicing the soles of Wasim's feet as he danced to shake the rats loose.

Bilqees held tight to her baby, dropping the stoker and trying to outrun the creature. It caught hold of her *dupatta*, however, yanking her head back. Bilqees stumbled into the wall, slamming her shoulder with such force into the concrete she feared her child might have taken a blow, too. Unfolding the swaddling to check was a mistake, however: the chuwa quickly stalked across the room and reached for the baby. Bilqees attempted to snatch the child from the monster's grasp, but a fraction too late. The chuwa's claws dug into the baby's soft flesh as it closed its grip, tearing across the infant's body as Bilqees wrested the child free.

The baby screamed so forcefully the rats were momentarily distracted from their torment of Wasim, and he shook them loose and sprinted across the room, sliding like one of those American baseball pitcher's he'd seen on television, knocking the legs out from under the chuwa towering over his wife. The creature went down, and suddenly there was his mother, standing over them both, a vase raised above her head. She brought it down into the chuwa's face, spilling blood. The chuwa hissed and thrashed on the floor, holding its hands over its eyes.

The other creature was over in a heartbeat, shoving Malika against the wall, knocking her dizzy. It reached down to seize Wasim and the boy covered his eyes with his arms, but the creature froze in the act, staring at Wasim's chest. The chuwa swiftly snatched the plane tickets from Wasim's shirt pocket, holding them up for study, blinking rapidly.

"Get away from my family!" roared Ansoor, charging at the creature from behind.

He jammed the fire stoker into the small of the chuwa's back, making it screech. The sound was certainly inhuman, and loud. The neighbours were bound to have woken by it, if not already from all the commotion. The stoker glowed red from the fire, and suddenly the creature's garments burst into flame, the fire licking up its back and singing the coarse hairs on its head.

Wasim uncovered his eyes to see the chuwa stumbling around the room, trying to beat at the flames on its back, but to no avail. Quickly it was consumed, the room hot with the conflagration. The horde of rats shrieked and fled, scuttling over the threshold and away into the Walled City's labyrinth laneways. He noticed the plane tickets on the floor, where he assumed they had fallen from his shirt pocket during the scuffle with the chuwa. He quickly picked them up just as the edge of the flames reached them.

Ansoor crawled across the floor to where his wife lay. The blind chuwa knelt but a few feet away, gasping and calling for its partner in crime. The screeching and the roar of the flames told it the errand was far from complete, and blindly it reached around until it had hold of Ansoor's foot, claws digging into the man's ankle, glancing off bone. Ansoor bellowed in agony.

"Abbu!" called Wasim, from the doorway, where he held his wife and baby. A wall of flame separated him from his parents.

"Go! Flee! More will come soon," said Ansoor, gasping with pain.

The chuwa was crawling across the rug toward him now, swearing bloody revenge.

Wasim's world tipped upside down. His own father and mother were about to be beset upon by a monster, and should he choose to brave the flames to rescue them, then he risked losing his wife and child to the creatures who would surely follow in the wake of this failed kidnapping.

"Go!" his father gasped, as the creature raised its arm, claws gleaming by the light of the fire.

Wasim's vision blurred from tears as he helped his bride out into the pale light of dawn, careful to make certain their baby was swaddled tight against the horrors of the world. Faces peered down from windows as he navigated the laneways, his feet leaving a tell-tale trail of blood. There were shouts behind him, calls for buckets of water, but he pressed on, determined his parents' deaths be not for naught.

For the umpteenth time, he felt with shaking fingers for the tickets in his shirt pocket, anxious to assure himself that he'd soon be away from the terrible events of this morning, and far away from the threat that lay in wait beneath his feet, deep underground.

CHAPTER 1

NOW

A hand reached up from the yawning expanse to grasp the cliff edge, knuckles bloodied, nails dirty and scuffed. A bob of messy blonde hair followed, as Jasmine Buckleigh hauled herself onto the cliff top, panting with exertion. Grime and sweat streamed down her face. She lay on her back gasping for breath, rubbing the blood from her knuckles on the tufts of dry grass growing between the cracks in the rocks.

A man appeared from over the cliff's edge, snarling at her, his arm slapping down on the rock, reaching for her.

Jasmine scuttled back, raising her foot, ready to kick out at the man.

"You wouldn't dare," the man said, pausing in his pursuit.

"I don't need to," Jasmine rejoined cockily, "I beat you fair and square."

The man, Raza Makhdoom, rested his forehead against the rock face in defeat.

"Rats," he cursed, finally lifting his hand in the air. "Help me the rest of the way, then."

Jasmine laughed, getting to her feet and hauling

Raza the remainder of the way. He fell onto the ground, belly up, shielding his eyes against the sun, legs tangled in the abseiling ropes.

"I swear, there's no-one faster or more nimble than you," he said between intakes of air.

Jasmine showed him her knuckles.

"But I always pay the price for it."

"Oh, *jannu*," Raza said, shifting tones and scrambling to his feet.

He took her hand in his, kissing her knuckles. She yanked her hand away, laughing.

"What are you, a vampire?" she taunted.

"Yeah, I vant to suuuck your bluuuud," he drawled in a hideous accent, pulling Jasmine closer, angling his mouth to her neck.

There came a curt clearing of throat, and Jasmine rolled her eyes to the sky and sighed, turning from Raza's embrace to face her mother.

Maureen Buckleigh stood beside the family car, holding up a wedding dress in one hand, and flashing a gold watch on her other.

"Really, Jasmine," she chastised, clucking her tongue, "of all the days, why rock climb on your wedding day?"

Behind Maureen was Raza's sister, Fouzia. She stepped forward, hands on hips, glaring at the groom-to-be.

"More's the point, brother, I thought it was traditional in both our cultures that the groom cannot see the bride on the marriage day!"

"Oh man, we're both getting grilled here," Raza murmured to Jasmine, and then to his sister he said: "*Aacha, aacha, baji-ji.* No problem. Relax."

Fouzia's nostrils flared.

"Relax? Look at you! Covered in dirt and sweat!"

"Come dear," Maureen Buckleigh said sniffily, slipping her arm through Fouzia's to lead the girl back to the car. "We'll wait in the car for the children to untangle themselves from their nonsense."

From the driver's side window, Jasmine's father Dan poked his head.

"Bring on the reception already, I say. Throat's as dry as a dead dingo's donger."

Maureen glared at her husband as she passed Fouzia the wedding dress through the rear door.

"Oh, really, Dan. Must you?"

Jasmine watched the exchange and, glancing momentarily at Raza and seeing his nose screw up at her father's tasteless analogy, burst into laughter.

"Welcome to the family!"

It had been intended to be a relatively humble reception in the back yard of Raza's family home, but the newlyweds had proven to be more popular than even they had reckoned on, and both the house and the yard were bustling with activity. Not a square foot of space was left unoccupied, and Raza's friends had made a trip down to the local liquor store for more supplies to keep the party going. Though Raza's parents abstained from alcohol for religious reasons, they weren't averse to their children assimilating with Australian norms.

But if the Buckleighs had been expecting the

Makhdooms to be modest with the festivities, then they were pleasantly surprised. Already, the revellers had been treated to two Bollywood-style dance numbers, one even led by the groom himself, Raza bedecked in jewelled *sherwani*. They had forsaken the traditional five days of marriage in favour of an afternoon ceremony, as befit the Australian custom, so the Makhdooms had been especially eager to leave their mark on the celebrations.

Outside, as the twilight gave way to night, a small boy of about ten years of age drummed to the delight of the crowd. The *dhol* was lashed to his waist, and his tiny hands beat furiously on the skin, sounding out a tattoo that got the feet of a few men moving. Zameer, Raza's friend since childhood, cleared a space betwixt the throng and the child, and tossing aside his jacket he proceeded to break-dance, spinning and twisting his body to the rhythm of the drumming. The boy whooped his encouragement, his hands working the *dhol* to a fever pitch as the onlookers roared in approval.

"Stand aside, joker boy," announced Fouzia, parting the crowd and grinning down at Zameer, who laughed and got to his feet, performing an elaborate bow to his challenger.

The child with the *dhol* smiled when Fouzia winked at him, and set his hands to beating out a fresh tempo, a hypnotic tumble of beats, as Fouzia began her *chaal*, a series of movements befitting the *dholi's* cadence. The crowd was in for a treat: the beat picked up speed, and Fouzia forsook the *chaal* in favour of a more frenetic dance style, mixing the martial style of dance called *baaga* with a contemporary edge, swinging her arms and lifting

14

her knees as she leaped around. She struck out at Zameer, as if to land a blow, and he fell back against his mates, laughing and cheering Fouzia on.

"Next marriage, Zameer and Fouzia," he announced to his friends at his back.

"Hey man, that's my sister you're talking about," came Raza's protest at his ear.

Zameer spun around to face his friend, laughing and slapping him on the chest.

"Relax, *bhai*. I'm only joking. Your sister is my sister also."

Fouzia reached over Zameer's shoulder and gave her brother a playful slap across the face. The crowd roared their approval, jibing Raza as Fouzia spun away again, arms swinging wildly to the beat of the drum.

"You know what?" Raza said to Zameer, shaking his head. "She's all yours. Marry her and take her far from me."

"I won't need to. When's your flight to the motherland again?"

"Next week," replied Raza. "Her first time in Pakistan."

He glanced through the doors to where Jasmine was chatting to guests in the kitchen, a flute of champagne spilling its contents as she waved her hand around animatedly. He smiled at the familiarity of it, having cleaned up after her on countless occasions when she was invested in a topic.

"And only then the marriage is final, *bhai*, remember that," Zameer said with a sly grin. "You're doing the *walima* there, still?"

Raza nodded. Conventionally, the *walima* was the final of the five days of wedding celebrations in

Pakistan, and though they'd forgone it all here in Australia, it had been decided they'd perform the last day – the *walima* – for old family back in Pakistan. Raza had only ever returned to the country of his birth a couple of times in all his years, and the family he had there were practically strangers to him. But they weren't to his parents, and it felt right to be doing this, to introduce Jasmine to his background, to square out their shared experiences moving forward.

"You're a lucky man," said Zameer softly, following Raza's train of sight to where the bride stood. "She'd go to the ends of the Earth for you."

"Yar. I know it, man," said Raza wistfully.

The celebrations continued into the night, winding down shortly before the eleventh hour. Jasmine's parents were the last to take their leave, Maureen facing her daughter at the front door and squeezing Jasmine's hands in her own, admiring the wedding ring on her daughter's finger a final time.

"We hope you have a wonderful time in Pakistan," Maureen said, unable to keep the note of anxiety creeping into her voice.

"We really do," Dan added, picking up on his wife's distress. After all, it wasn't an ideal holiday destination as far as they were concerned. But it was where the kids had decided to honeymoon, so be it.

"We'll be fine, Mum, seriously," Jasmine smiled, pulling her mother into an embrace. "It's only two weeks. It'll be an exciting adventure, to see where Raza was born."

Wasim Makhdoom, Raza's father, shared a glance with his wife, though no-one in the room caught it.

"Well, we're happy it will be to our motherland," enthused Bilqees, Raza's mother. "We miss it so much, ever since we left."

"I'm sure you do," Maureen said, looking sympathetically at Bilqees. "And if Raza's grandmother is as hospitable as you are, dear, then I'm more worried about Jasmine coming home having outgrown her wardrobe."

Titters all round at the joke, then Bilqees took Jasmine's head gently in her hands, tilting it down to place her nose on Jasmine's hairline.

"Bless you, *dulhan*. You have made us very happy."

Maureen sniffled, rummaging amongst the litter in her handbag to fetch a tissue.

Dan Buckleigh looked bemused by his wife.

"What's gotten into you?"

Maureen turned away to delicately blow her nose.

"Oh, you know how I get at weddings; I turn into such an emotional mess."

Bilqees Makhdoom laughed. "Bless you, too, dear."

The couples made their farewells, Jasmine's parents taking their leave before she retired upstairs to finish packing her suitcase for the plane trip in the morning.

Wasim watched his daughter-in-law disappear around the bend at the top of the stairs, and turned to his son, his wistful expression darkening.

"Now remember what to do if there's any trouble, son."

"Of course," Raza nodded. "Call you and follow Aunty Malika's instructions. But, *papa-ji*, I've been there twice now and nothing is wrong. Why do you keep insisting something bad can happen?"

Wasim averted his eyes to the floor.

"I'm just saying, you know," he said, quietly.

Raza looked at him askance, as he began to ascend the stairs to check on Jasmine.

"Yeah, you're always *just saying* that when I go back to Pakistan for a visit. It's not *that* bad, *abbu*. You must remember, surely?"

Wasim smiled sadly and waved Raza away, as if to suggest he was only being silly with his fears.

In Raza's bedroom, Jasmine was knelling on her suitcase to flatten in more.

"Kind of nervous, got to admit," Jasmine said, as Raza helped with the zip on her suitcase. "It'll be my first time abroad, let alone Pakistan."

"You think the celebrations here are mad," grinned Raza, "just wait until you see them Pak style."

"What's it called again, this reception we'll have there?"

"The *walima*."

Jasmine rolled the word over and over on her tongue, enjoying the sound. She watched as her husband (a designation she'd already become comfortable with) peeled off his shirt, rubbing absent-mindedly at an old scar running across his stomach from side to side.

"Old wound playing up again?"

Raza nodded.

"How'd you get it again?"

"Rolled over when I was a baby," said Raza, casually. "Fan cut me."

"Sounds like your parents were trying to bump you off," laughed Jasmine.

"Yeah, yeah, very funny."

Glancing up, she saw he wasn't amused by her

playfulness, but she couldn't help poking the hornet's nest. It was always in her nature.

"Oh, poor baby," she teased, crossing to him and catching him in a hug from behind. "I didn't mean to make fun of you."

"Sure you didn't," he said, losing the irritated tone.

"You doubt me?"

Raza gave it some thought, listening intently for the telltale intake of air which signalled Jasmine's self-righteousness, anticipating her switch into defensiveness. It was their little thing, pushing each other's boundaries, as they had earlier in the day whilst rock-climbing, competing to see who could make the top first.

"You bet I do," he said quickly, to catch her off-guard.

But she was quick, his bride, countering without missing a heartbeat.

"In that case..."

Raza felt his feet lift the floor as Jasmine hefted him, throwing him sideways onto the bed. The room blurred, then the soft landing face-first into the doona cover, pulling forth the joy of childhood memories when his sister Fouzia would wrestle him down into the pillows, loudly claiming her victory.

He spun his body, feeling Jasmine's weight shift, forcing her to fall into the space he'd previously occupied. He was now the victor, lying across her as she cursed him and kicked her feet furiously. He began tickling her sides to infuriate her more, until tears ran from her eyes, her face red from laughter.

"Wait... wait!"

Raza stopped the torture.

"Wait why?"

Jasmine grunted. "Wedding dresses aren't made for wrestling in."

Raza let her up, undoing the zip on her back. The dress peeled away, and Raza gently ran his fingers down her naked spine. She shivered visibly.

"Do more of that," Jasmine demanded, her voice melting into a satisfied moan.

"Keep it down; my parents are out there somewhere."

"We're legal now, so they better have earplugs," said Jasmine, turning to him with a devilish smirk.

"Don't you even dare," warned Raza, worry and humour comingling in his expression.

Jasmine buried her face in his shoulder to stifle her hilarity.

CHAPTER 2

When Jasmine stepped from Allama Iqbal International Airport, the city of Lahore struck its first blow. She was delivered into a congested crowd of men, crammed around the airport doors and jostling for view of arrivals. Almost as a singular entity they stared hard at her, at her pale skin and her long yellow hair. And before she'd had time to take stock of this situation and steel herself against it, Jasmine was rudely shoved forward by an impatient – or perhaps careless? – lady behind her

Jasmine had no time to consider it, for she'd been propelled into the reach of the staring throng, the sea of men parting enough for her to lose herself amongst them, closing behind her so the airport disappeared from view. Immediately she felt a hand on her breast, groping gracelessly, seizing upon the opportunity while the anonymity of the crowd afforded it. Who was the culprit? Jasmine was spinning now, seeing only a wall of lusty faces and hearing a cacophony of strange sounds, a language she couldn't understand.

Suddenly, there was Raza, her Raza. He took Jasmine by the arms and stilled her, turned her to him and caught her eyes with his own.

"It's okay, calm down. Just breathe."

She didn't mention the wandering hand, of its

pressure still felt on her breast. The crowd of men had stepped back to afford her some breathing space, probably because of Raza's arrival. It annoyed Jasmine the way Raza now studied her, how ignorant he was of the men pressing around her, suffocating her, touching her.

"I'm fine, it's hot, is all," she replied tersely, turning away.

They fought through the press of men until they cleared the other side. No sooner were they free of the melee than they were beset upon by more men, yelling for attention.

"*Goree! Goree!* Over here! You come!"

Another man appeared by her side, as if by a magician's trick.

"Miss Yellow! *Chelo!*" he entreated, pointing toward the carpark.

Raza waved his hand at the man, casually barking an order at him. It didn't deter the man, who kept calling Jasmine "Miss Yellow".

If Jasmine had been in any doubt as to the basis of the man's nickname, it was dispelled when a young woman they passed abruptly reached out to take a handful of Jasmine's hair, sliding it between her calloused fingers.

"*Bas! Bas!*" shouted Raza, and the woman pulled her hand back as if physically struck, straightening her *dupatta* while looking indignantly at Raza.

Though Raza was telling the woman to leave them be, it sounded to Jasmine like he was asking directions for the bus, which she could see at the far end of the terminal. So naturally she assumed the big-bellied man with greying hair and a brown *shalwar-kameez* propped against a brick post and nodding at

Raza was a bus-driver. A quick exchange in Urdu secured the man's services. Money was exchanged in advance, and by sleight of hand the rupee notes disappeared into the folds of the man's clothing before Jasmine realised it had happened. He directed them toward a tiny yellow Suzuki Alto with TAXI emblazoned on the side in English, roughly taking their luggage and cramming it in the rear hatch.

Though dusty inside the taxi – upholstery ripped and unwashed – Jasmine felt relief wash over her. The chaos of the airport, the faces staring at her, the shouting in a language she couldn't comprehend, it had all been too much, too soon. A ride on a bus would have only exacerbated her anxiety. As if reading the situation, Raza climbed in next to her, looking pensive.

"Sorry, but there was no way to prepare you for this," he offered. "I just hoped for the best."

Jasmine let out a sigh.

"Oh, great... thanks," she mumbled sarcastically.

A pang of remorse struck her when Raza's face fell and he began conversing with the driver in Urdu. Jasmine wished she'd taken up lessons to learn the language back when Fouzia had offered. In truth, she had guessed a little of what to expect when the plane had descended into Lahore, the flight path cutting across miles and miles of densely packed city. Even from the air, she'd spied the congested traffic crawling along narrow streets, the wider main roads a constant flow of trucks and motorbikes. And nor had any vista been without its share of people, scurrying amongst the city's lanes and streets like a nest of agitated ants. The population would be dense, that much had been obvious. That it *had been* directly at the doors of the airport had simply come as a culture shock.

The driver turned the engine off while they waited at the intersection for the lights to turn green.

"To save on fuel–" Raza began to explain when he saw the panic in Jasmine's eyes, but he was cut short by a thumping against her window.

Jasmine yelped out loud, half-leaping across the seat towards Raza. The driver cursed, having seen what bothered his passengers. He growled angrily out his window.

Peering in through the grimy glass was a small face. Jasmine might have even thought it cute, but for the dried snot clogging the child's nose and the festering sores on its neck. The child, a small boy of about eight years old, leaned back then rammed his forehead against the glass window.

"Did he just head-butt the window?" Jasmine asked incredulously.

"He's trying to get us to open it," Raza said.

There was also a boy at his window, ready to bang his head against the glass.

"*Bas!*" Raza yelled.

"What's wrong with them? What do they want?"

The driver mumbled something unintelligible, though he was watching Jasmine in his rear-view mirror. Though he sounded angry, his eyes were sad.

"I shouldn't do this," Raza mumbled, fishing a couple of crumpled rupee notes from his wallet and winding the squeaky window down.

"Then maybe you shouldn't?" Jasmine said, unsure of what was actually happening.

When Raza reached out to poke the money into a plastic bag tied around the boy's neck, she saw there

were two mangled stumps poking from the sleeves of his filthy tee-shirt. She snapped her head around to peer out her own window, and saw similarly the boy on her side was missing his arms.

"Beggars," she heard the driver say, and glanced up to see his eyes boring into her via the mirror. He held up a cupped hand, as to ask for spare change. "For mafia." Then he flattened his palm and made a chopping motion in the air.

"No way," gasped Jasmine, returning to stare at the boy at her window.

The flesh of his arms was twisted at the end, as though a botched surgery had been performed. The boy hadn't been born limbless, she knew. The driver's assessment was spot on: these small children had had their arms cut off, probably by an axe.

She shuddered, feeling her skin go cold.

"*Allahu akbar*," said the boy at Raza's window, in a voice devoid of feeling.

Raza returned the blessing, rolling his window up as the lights turned green and the taxi moved out into the slipstream of traffic on the Lahore Ring Road.

"Those boys, begging," Jasmine heard herself saying numbly. "It's not right."

"It isn't," Raza agreed cautiously. "But there's nothing for it, babe. The mafias are powerful here. There's a lot of corruption. Try not to focus on it, okay."

Jasmine looked at her husband as though he had two heads.

"They shouldn't be out here in the traffic, begging for money. They should be looked after, with their families."

Raza sighed impatiently.

"Yeah, agreed. But they could be orphans of war, or abandoned, or could be slaves. Could be anything. We can't do much about it."

"Slaves," Jasmine repeated, the word as alien on her tongue as any in Urdu. "Slaves?"

The driver was watching her in the mirror, and she wondered how he could navigate the crazy traffic when he never seemed to have his eyes on the road.

"I just want us to have a good time here, you know?" said Raza. "There's lots of interesting and fun things about Lahore. You'll see."

Jasmine wasn't convinced.

"Okay. But it better get more fun than this, I'm telling you."

"It will," assured Raza, trying a small smile and finally receiving one in return.

"Still insane, though," Jasmine said, shaking her head as she watched the city slip by.

"Hey, no argument here," Raza rejoined, directing the driver to take several turns at various landmarks.

"Can't just give him the address?" Jasmine asked.

Raza shook his head.

"Grandma moved to a new area. The streets don't even have names yet, let alone the entire suburb."

Jasmine started laughing, despite herself.

"Sorry," she said when Raza raised a brow. "Sounds like we're headed to Nowheresville."

The trip continued for another half hour, though at one point Jasmine could swear they'd actually double-backed, whilst Raza was adamant they hadn't. The roads were choked with all manner of obstacle: whole families piled onto a single motorbike; brick-laden wooden carts angled so workers could easily shift the load, whilst the small donkey tethered to the bamboo shafts hung in the air like a ragdoll, straining in its leather harness; bustling mosques of gleaming blue tile right beside a greasy mechanic's shop, the condition of garments of patrons to either in stark contrast with one another; a herd of beetal goats creating a traffic jam at one point, their impossibly long ears flapping as their shepherds rushed them between the tight spaces between cars and buses to the other side of the road.

By the time they reached their destination, Jasmine was fatigued from sensory overload. Meeting Raza's grandmother for the first time was a big deal, though, so she quickly unclasped her makeup mirror and tidied herself up. She wanted to be as presentable as possible and leave a good impression. If she knew anything from having spent time with Raza's family in Australia, she knew first impressions were of the utmost importance here.

The taxi left in a burst of exhaust smoke just as Raza's grandmother opened the metal door to her home. True to Jasmine's speculation, the woman was done up to the nines, or in what Jasmine's father would have described as "her Sunday best." Hair coifed, gold jewellery shining in the sunlight, power-suit pressed (though old-fashioned in design by modern standards). In her hands she held a bludgeoning club of solid wood.

Instinctively Jasmine drew back from the armed woman. She couldn't be sure, but there appeared to be blood on the end of the club.

"Hello, *dadi*," said Raza reverently.

The old woman narrowed her eyes, glancing up and down the street, but for signs of what Jasmine could only guess at. The arrival of a foreigner to the neighbourhood hadn't gone unnoticed, and where some children had been playing in a doorway across the street there now stood a whole family, smiling and waving to Jasmine. Tentatively, she returned the gesture, keeping an eye on the eccentric old woman with the club. Seemingly satisfied there was no threat, Raza's grandmother beckoned them forward.

"Quick! Inside!"

Raza grinned at Jasmine, unperturbed by the woman's alarming behaviour.

"C'mon, let's get this stuff in quickly," he said, hefting both their suitcases.

Jasmine followed him up the steps, careful not to tread on the smooth incline of concrete running up their centre, which Raza explained was a ramp to drive a scooter inside. Jasmine glanced back and realised there were no parking garages, that the other homes had huge metal doors opening into their lounge where cars could be parked.

The door clanged shut behind them, plunging them into darkness. The sound of bolts sliding into position made Jasmine nervous, so she positioned Raza between herself and the door. If the crazy old bat was going to attack, she might be less inclined to do so with her own grandson standing between them.

"Raza?"

She felt his hand squeeze her own, comforted by his touch. Beyond where he must have stood, a long, dark corridor stretched, at the end of which a room spilled enough light to reveal an older man watching them at the end of the hall. His spectacles glinted in the feeble light when he inclined his head. But this man was the least of Jasmine's concerns at present;

she glanced around, her eyes gradually adjusting to the gloom enough to make out the old woman standing her wooden club against the wall beside the door.

"Come," she said.

Raza took Jasmine's hand and pulled her along, following the old woman into the next room where the light from a stairwell revealed decorations of vases, paintings, ornate timber furniture, and a beautiful rug stretching to all corners of the room.

The old woman turned to face them, smiling and opening her arms. Raza bowed his head before her, as the old woman ran her hands over his hair, muttering.

"Good to see you again, my dearest grandson. How are you?"

Without waiting for an answer, the old woman turned to Jasmine with a smile.

"So, this is her?"

Without meaning to, Jasmine looked fleetingly back through the arch to where the wooden club stood in the gloom. The old woman caught the glance, her face creasing with impish glee.

"For rats," she squeaked.

Jasmine nodded her head slowly, which made Raza laugh out loud.

"She'll do," said the old woman. "You've married well enough, my grandson. May you have many sons."

"Oh, great, thanks," snorted Jasmine.

"You can call me Malika," the old woman smiled, patting Jasmine's hand. "Sit. I'll make tea."

She went through another archway, and when Jasmine could hear the kettle being filled, she took a deep breath and expelled it, feeling her muscles relax a little. Raza plopped himself down on the floor, crossing his legs.

"Okay, that was weird," Jasmine said, sitting next to him.

He proffered her a cushion, which she accepted.

"She's just eccentric. Always has been. But it's quiet here, at least. All the homes of my other relatives are bursting with a dozen screaming kids each."

"But what was that business with the club? Scared the daylights out of me."

"The rats?" Raza chuckled lightly. "She's mortally afraid of rats. Has been ever since I've known her. Don't worry about it."

"Don't laugh," scoffed Jasmine. "I honestly thought she was going to hit me with it."

Raza burst into uncontrollable laughter, slapping his knee.

"If she doesn't approve, she chases you away!"

Jasmine glared at him, but unable to maintain her dissatisfaction at his amusement she started to laugh along.

Malika carried in a tray of tea in china cups and a plate of biscuits. She grinned broadly, as though sharing their joke.

"Oh, it's good to have fun in the house again. It's been too long since, living on my own."

Jasmine couldn't help but raise an eyebrow at this last remark, remembering the man with the spectacles in the hallway earlier. Whilst Raza helped himself, Malika passed a cup of tea to Jasmine.

"*Jannu...*" she said, the teacup rattling on the plate as her shaky hands passed the tea across.

Jasmine thanked the old woman.

"*Meribani*" said Malika, in tone suggesting Jasmine was being corrected.

"Sorry?"

"This is how we say *thank-you* in Urdu," said Malika. *"Meribani."*

Jasmine nodded her head. She knew the word, Raza's father having taught it to her for fun, but with the stress of the day's events she'd momentarily forgotten.

"Oh yes," she nodded. *"Meribani."*

Malika tittered.

"Ooh, her Urdu is good," she said to her grandson, sincerely. "And what is your program in Pakistan?"

"We have no plans for today, *dadi*," Raza answered. "Just relax from the flight, *hai'na*? Maybe take Jasmine for a sight-see of Lahore tomorrow morning."

Malika nodded.

"Your cousin will be available then, he can drive you on his motorbike."

"Nah, I'd prefer it to be just Jasmine and myself at first. We'll take a rickshaw. Do it Lahori style, *hai'na*?"

Malika smiled sweetly at Jasmine.

"That is so romantic."

Jasmine gave an exaggerated and insincere smile in return, sipping her tea. Unaware of Jasmine's growing discomfort, Raza asked his grandmother if it was still okay to have their wedding reception – the *walima* – on the roof of her home.

"You know, this is my honour," said Malika, hand over her heart. "And everyone will be so jealous of me because of Australia company here in my home."

"Great," laughed Raza. "I'll go tomorrow and get

the invites from Uncle's print shop at Anarkali Bazaar, do the rounds of inviting everyone."

Malika beamed at Jasmine.

"You have brought such happiness and hope to our whole family!"

Such was the sincerity of the old woman's enthusiasm, Jasmine finally relented and felt herself relax, enjoying the warmth of the tea-cup in her palms.

"And damn all the rats!" Malika nearly shouted, making Jasmine jump and spill her tea.

Raza yanked a fistful of tissues from on the coffee-table and helped mop up the tea dribbling over Jasmine's arm, dabbing at the wet cushion. Malika rose to her feet, looking triumphant, oblivious to the clean-up operation right at her feet. Glancing up at her, Jasmine couldn't help but think how heroic the old woman stood, chest out, chin held high, staring proudly at a photo on the wall of an old man, presumably Raza's grandfather. Noticing Jasmine's bemused expression, Raza began to snicker, struggling not to laugh out loud. His shaking shoulders betrayed the effort as he buried his face against his chest to stifle his hilarity.

"For celebration tonight," Malika continued, "I am cooking a special dinner. Delicious *paow.*"

"*Paow?*" Jasmine gaped, cocking a brow.

"Goats' feet stew," Raza explained, choking as he nearly burst into a fresh round of laughter at Jasmine's horrified expression.

"What do you say to that?" Malika beamed, hands on hips.

Jasmine wasn't sure what to say, looking to Raza for guidance, but her husband chose to be of no use, simply hiding his head under a cushion as he continued to find entertainment in her discomfort.

"Meribani?" Jasmine ventured uncertainly.

Malika clapped her hands together like a whip-crack, cackling hysterically.

CHAPTER 3

The gloom of the chamber shifted, the shadows congealing to form mass from vacant air. Or rather, the shadows shifted to *reveal*, rather than construct. The gloom was a facade, and from behind it emerged the terrifying Bride, her brightly coloured veil obscuring her face. Huge, gold loop-earrings glinted from the folds.

Likewise, the creature standing before her had removed his own disguise, flipping back the scarf from his face, if for any reason than for the heat. Sweat poured down his face and neck. Though he appeared human, Pirak's features put that notion to the test, with his black eyes and twitching muzzle, the medial cleft more animal than not. He was chuwa through and through, one of the infamous rat-people of Lahore. A jagged patch of pale, hairless flesh – the mark of vitiligo Pirak had had since his birth – marred the side of his face. When he licked his lips nervously, bucked teeth reached down to his bottom lip.

There was a third presence in the chamber, trembling in the bestial grip of the creature. The child couldn't have been more than eight years old, and though her cheeks were still wet from tears shed, presently they'd dried up to be replaced with sheer terror at the looming sight of the Bride.

"This is... promising, chuwa," the Bride's voice sang, the chamber resounding with her baritone.

Pirak nodded eagerly.

"I see..." the Bride continued, sighing irritably

when her audience whined in anticipation of her revelations. "I see things coming full circle for you, chuwa."

"The war for territories?" Pirak's voice was reedy and unpleasant. "We get control of Lahore?"

"You will."

The creature grinned broadly, exposing a full set of deadly incisors.

"Kha'i will be pleased with this news."

"But..."

Pirak's face fell, his grip tightening on the terrified child.

"You will win, and you may lose," the Bride said cryptically. "Another will challenge you all, each and every one of you. A man marked, and a woman with hair of the sun. They are destruction."

The chuwa's eyes narrowed, his tongue darting across his lip.

"Yet you said we will win, Bride. We will have control?"

The shadows deepened, obscuring the Bride momentarily. Pirak couldn't help moaning in anguish, thinking his audience with her had come to a perplexing end.

"Yes, Jamallan, you will," the shadows finally confirmed.

"It is the only news I have interest of, then," Pirak said. "The offering, as usual."

The creature shoved the child forward, her bare feet scuffing on the stone floor as she resisted. He kicked at the back of her knees, forcing her to drop to floor. The gloom became agitated, wafting toward the girl.

"We will be back again for more good news, in time," Pirak promised, turning away as he wrapped his scarf around his head to hide his features.

The darkness parted, and the Bride pushed through as if birthed from it. Her pallid and cracked lips, snaked with thick brown veins, broke into a small smile.

"Heed the warnings, chuwa," she whispered. "Heed them well."

Pirak paused in the stairwell, glancing over his shoulder a final time at the Bride. He shrugged, ascending the steps two at a time.

"Now, child," the Bride said, peeling back the layers of gloom concealing her true form, a furnace-like heat filling the air.

The little girl finally found her voice, screaming in terror.

CHAPTER 4

The bones were greasy yellow, the meat gnawed away until only the cartilage remained between the joints. They were piled in pools of stagnant stew on their plates. Malika had excused herself partway through the meal to prepare dessert in the kitchen, and Raza had taken the opportunity to play with his mobile phone. Reception in Pakistan was terrible, and he hadn't been able to make or receive any calls or texts since arriving, despite having done his research on the best possible plans before leaving Australia. He notched it up to having fallen for the false promises of the marketing men, deciding to add a visit to a phone shop in the morrow's plans.

Malika entered the room, carrying a tray laden with three bowls and accompanying spoons. Jasmine helped clear the plates, despite Malika's insistence she shouldn't bother herself. Noting the heaped bones on Jasmine's plate, the old woman smiled proudly.

"Did you enjoy the goats' feet, Jasmine-ji?"

"They were lovely," Jasmine lied, inspecting the fresh bowl set before her. It looked like white custard, spices sprinkled on top.

"Ooh, I'll have to cook them again for you," Malika beamed.

Jasmine grimaced at the prospect.

When Malika had vanished again to the kitchen, talking to herself, Raza furrowed his brow.

"You ate the goats' feet?"

"No, the bones were from your plate," Jasmine smirked. "I nicked some when you weren't looking."

Raza lifted the lid of the pot, and saw it was empty. Only an inch of stew water remained, bubbles of oil congealing on its surface.

"Wait, so where'd your serve go, then?"

Jasmine bashfully patted her sides.

"Get out," Raza gasped. "You put your goats' feet in your cardigan pockets?"

He started laughing just as his grandmother returned.

"Malika, what's this dish?" Jasmine asked, hoping to distract the old woman from enquiring as to the joke.

"*Kheer*, dear," Malika replied, tittering at her own joke. "*Kheer* is rice pudding."

"Not good for pockets," Raza blurted, almost falling backwards from laughing so hard.

Jasmine slapped his leg, and then remembering in whose house she was, smiled brightly at Malika and spooned the pudding into her mouth. This dish, she liked. Malika turned the television on while they ate, absorbed by an Indian drama.

"Come on, Raza, help me," whispered Jasmine. "They're wet. My cardigan's going to stink forever now."

"Well, you can't put them in the bin," he said, shaking his head. "My grandmother will see them."

"I wish I could give it to those poor boys at the airport. I feel bad about how I reacted."

Raza slurped noisily at his dessert, lost in thought.

"You know," he finally said, slowly, "I think there are homeless people in the laneway outside."

Jasmine cocked her head, her eyes going wide.

"Yes! Can I give it to them?"

"Sure, why not? I'll meet you at the front door."

When she'd finished her *kheer*, Jasmine collected the other bowls, pleading with Malika to sit and enjoy her television show. From the kitchen, she slipped through a side arch into the darkness of a hallway, mentally mapping out the route to the front door. From there, she could see through to the lounge where the old woman sat entranced by the theatrics on-screen. The goat's feet in her pockets had begun to cool, the gravy of their meat turning to slime, so she slid them out, holding them gingerly. She screwed her nose up at their touch, repulsed.

A noise beside her caught her attention, and expecting Raza to sidle up to her in the murk she turned to come face-to-face with a naked man. His skin was so dark he was practically invisible, save for the whites of his eyes staring impassively at her.

Jasmine screamed, dropping the goats' feet on the floor, where they bounced, landing on her toes and startling her again. She shook them off, pressing herself against the door with her fists in the air to ward off the intruder in the dark.

Raza appeared, silhouetted in the archway.

"Jasmine!"

The man was stone-still, staring at her. He gave her the impression of being unbothered by the commotion, or of her husband's advent. Raza rushed forward, stepping between his wife and the interloper, holding a hand out to ward the man off

41

even though he stood motionless.

"Who are you?" Raza demanded.

The man gave no response, so Raza switched over to Urdu, repeating his interrogation. The man waggled his head and gave a short reply.

"He said he's catching rats," Raza translated.

From behind the man, another appeared in the hallway. For the first time Jasmine could see neither man was actually naked: they wore the *shameez* pants, and were topless. The new arrival even carried a small cage and a *lathi*. And neither of them was the geriatric she'd spied when she'd first arrived; each were easily half that particular man's age.

Malika had stolen away from her broadcast dramas upon hearing the urgency of the one breaking out in her own home.

"It's okay, *pota-ji*," she said to her grandson. "They are the rat-catchers. They come once a week."

Raza dropped his defences, relaxing.

"Like pest exterminators?"

Raza greeted the men, who nodded in return. They remained humourless, staring at Jasmine as though she were an apparition. Raza indicted a bottle one of the men carried, and they opened it for him to smell.

"Whoo, babe, that's strong stuff," he chuckled to Jasmine, waving his hand before his face. "A strong blend of wheat, poison and garlic in that."

"And what's in there?" Jasmine said, pointing at a tin bucket the other man carried.

"Water," Malika offered. "To drown the rats they catch."

Jasmine shivered, imagining the men coolly plunging the little cage into the bucket of water until the thrashing of their captives ceased. While her grandmother-in-law conferred with the men on their progress, Jasmine discreetly crouched down to retrieve the goats' feet from the floor, keeping them behind her back lest Malika notice.

"You should have told us they were here, *dadi*," said Raza to his grandmother. "I was about to hurt these guys something fierce. And they gave poor Jasmine a scare."

"They are harmless," Malika protested.

Jasmine smiled uncomfortably, her grip on the slimy goats' feet beginning to slip.

"Unless you're a rat, of course," added Malika with a cackle.

Jasmine glanced at Raza uncertainly, who smiled and shrugged.

"*Aacha, dadi*, we're going to take some air now," said Raza, sliding back the bolts on the door.

The rat-catcher closest to Jasmine leant slightly to one side, his eyes dropping to Jasmine's rear. Instinctively she glared at him, realising only then that the man was looking quizzically at the goat's feet dripping in her hands. She shook her head, shushing him as faintly as she could. He stood erect and glanced away.

"Oh, are you feeling okay?" Malika enquired of Jasmine, whose heart began beating furiously, thinking she'd been caught out in her deception.

"Yeah, we're fine, *dadi*," Raza interjected, "just nice to take a little walk after a big meal. *Hai'na?*"

Malika nodded, and turning to the rat-catchers, she snapped: "Why are you just standing here? Eliminated every rat in Lahore already, have you? Go on, back to work."

The air outside wasn't fresh, but it was a welcome change. Jasmine ruminated how with so much diesel pollution in Lahore, smoking was a pointless habit. The streets were no less vacant for the night, either: if anything, they were busier. People jostled for space along the streets with all manner of vehicles. Though the buses hadn't abated, there was a far greater amount of cars and motorbikes than during the day. Their headlights streamed through the dust and exhaust fumes.

"Are the rest of your Pakistan family as strange as your grandmother?" Jasmine said, dodging the potholes of piss and mud.

"She's unique," Raza said warmly. "She's my favourite relative."

"I don't know," Jasmine ventured carefully. "She said she lives alone, but there was a man with glasses when we first arrived."

"You saying my grandmother's got a secret lover stashed away in the house?" laughed Raza.

Jasmine shrugged. "Maybe. He was about twenty years younger, I'd guess."

Raza laughed even harder. "Now you're calling my grandmother a cougar!"

"You know, these are getting pretty difficult to hold onto," complained Jasmine, the goats' feet at arm's length in case they fell against her clothing.

"Just down here," he promised, leading the way around the corner into a tight space, a lane extending into unfathomable darkness. It stank of trash and rotting waste, and of human excrement. Jasmine pressed her nose into the sleeve of her cardigan, trying not to gag from the smell. Raza kept his nostrils pinched with one hand.

"There should be some homeless people down here," he said, his voice high and squeaky.

Jasmine wanted to laugh, but dared not, and the gloom before her had begun to fill her with trepidation. She began to wonder at the wisdom of her new husband, leading them astray into this shit-filled alleyway at night.

"Maybe we should wait until morning," Jasmine said, her voice muffled.

"If you want to," Raza said.

It was too dark to read his expression, but she imagined she heard a hint of disappointment in his voice. They'd been friends for years before getting married, and what had bonded them was their shared passion for adventure and excitement. They'd hiked mountains, camped in remote forests, swum rivers untouched by modern civilisation. In her mind's eye she saw the little boys at the airport, plastic bags tied around their necks, the mangled stumps of their arms waving at their sides like underdeveloped wings. From their backs she imagined the same boys sprouting magnificent wings, covered in the purest feathers, beating so powerfully they repelled the men who watched their every movement, who coveted them for their value to extort sympathy. She imagined the boys taking flight, rising above the melee and the smog of Lahore until they were soaring the clean blue skies, free and without suffering.

"No," Jasmine said firmly. "It's now or never."

She pushed past Raza, striding confidently into the darkness of the lane, feeling her way with her feet. The trash piled along the walls closed in the further she went, but she was determined.

"Hello!" she called. "Is anyone in there?"

A rustle told her she was not alone. She glanced back, and Raza stood but a few paces away, encouraging her with a nod. Beyond him, the relative safety of the street, the spotlights mounted to storefronts flaring in the dust. She calculated it was a good fifty paces to reach, and should whatever lie in the darkness decide to fling itself screeching at Jasmine, she knew she'd be in trouble.

"Listen, I have some food here," she announced nervously.

With effort, she could make out movement ahead, watching as a great shape rose up, standing easily a few feet taller than she. Jasmine took a step back, her muscles straining. She proffered the food, holding it high in front of her.

"Please, it's for you," she said.

Another step back.

The great shape lumbered toward her, kicking trash from its path in its progress, advancing with a speed belying its size.

"Raza?"

His voice returned her enquiry. She could hear he was right behind her.

The darkness ahead softened, until a bear of a man advanced close enough for the spill of light from the street to pick his features from the gloom at his back. He was huge, towering above Jasmine, with a tangle of beard reaching down to his belly. Dressed only in a tattered *shalwar-kameez*, a vest and *kakaul* fashioned from cardboard completing his look. Despite the condition of his attire, the man was imposing.

He sniffed the air.

"Paow?"

His voice was deep and kindly. Jasmine could tell that if the man so desired, he could roar with enough power to instil fear in the entire neighbourhood, yet he contained himself.

"What?" said Jasmine, her mouth agape with wonder.

The big man pointed at the food in her hands.

"Oh, yes, yes, *paow*," she stammered.

He removed the *kakaul* from his head, a show of respect as uncommon as it was absurd in the trash-filled back-alleys of South Asia.

"Yes, here," Jasmine said, lowering the offering, stretching it as far from herself as she could.

The man approached timidly, and likewise stretched his arms forward, mimicking Jasmine's pose. He turned his cardboard hat upside down in parody of a bowl.

"Oh, but your hat, it'll turn to mush," Jasmine said, and assuming the man couldn't understand her, she looked back to Raza for translation, which he did so happily.

"It is okay," the big man returned, in English.

Jasmine crept forward, tipping the goats' feet into the cardboard bowl.

"*Shukriya*," the man said softly, straightening slowly to his full height.

Jasmine found herself tilting her head back to look up at him. He was a mammoth of a man, but the gentlest of giants, it seemed. She turned and made her way back to Raza, shielding her eyes against the glare of the street. When she reached him, she turned to consider the homeless man again, but he was gone, having been swallowed by the darkness of the narrow lane. His voice, however, deep and beautiful, reached back to them, and translating, Raza told her the man had a companion back there, possibly a wife, and he was sharing the food with her.

"I feel better now," Jasmine confessed. "I haven't wasted your grandmother's cooking."

Raza smiled, wrapping an arm around Jasmine's shoulder.

"Good," he said simply, guiding her from the alley and back onto the street.

They made their way home, marvelling at the dexterity required to avoid colliding with either pedestrian or vehicle. As they made to go upstairs, they saw Malika working in the kitchen, cutting beans for the following days' meals. Raza poked his head around the corner.

"Hey, *Dadi*, we're going to retire for the night and sleep some of this jetlag off."

"*Shab-bakhair*," the old woman said.

As the couple started up the stairs, the old woman raised her voice to be heard.

"I daresay after such a tasty meal those homeless people will need a good sleep, too."

Jasmine stopped, her hand on the rail, and stared in horror at Raza. He stared back before grinning, which made her break into a stifled giggle, and they raced up the stairs to cover their embarrassment.

In the kitchen, Malika chuckled to herself as she brought the knife down on a fistful of beans, cleanly slicing off their ends.

CHAPTER 5

Lahore was unlike anything Jasmine knew, and certainly not a city she'd ever have dreamt of visiting. It was chaos and charm at once: the terrifying ride in an auto-rickshaw as elaborately-painted trucks bore down either side, their shrill whistles and horns nearly deafening her; holding her breath each time they passed by a smouldering pile of rubbish and dung roadside, plunging headlong into the pungent tendrils of smoke and emerging beyond, hoping there were no vehicles or pedestrians lingering on the other side of the smoke; spotting mausoleums and mosques and trying to differentiate between the two, so grand were each.

Even the apparently simple act of procuring a rickshaw to transport them around proved to be something of an adventure. Raza had quickly caught on that the drivers (*rickshaw-wallahs*, he'd called them) were hiking the prices skyward on account of Jasmine's presence, as a foreigner, so he decided to play a little game with them. Having been to see Zamzama, also known as Kim's Gun after Kipling's child protagonist, Raza asked Jasmine to wait discreetly behind a pole.

She was a little apprehensive standing alone, watching Raza stride confidently toward a small convoy of parked rickshaws and striking up a conversation with the men who lounged in them, smoking languidly. She could see Raza laughing with them, making a lot of hand gestures, some of which she easily read. It was obvious he was haggling to get the fare lowered.

From behind she could hear mumbling, and was startled to discover someone crawling on the ground toward her, mouth agape, matted hair hanging in front of their eyes. For a moment she thought it something undead, risen inexplicably in broad daylight on the busy streets of Pakistan to reach out for her soul. After all, the man appeared to be shorn in half, and how could any human survive such a thing? But on closer inspection, she saw he was sat upon a board with castors nailed to the underside, wheeling himself around by clawing at the ground. His legs poked uselessly from under the rags he wore.

"I'm sorry," Jasmine said instinctively, unsure what to do.

The man stopped near her feet, holding a hand up and mumbling to himself.

Jasmine glanced back at Raza, but he was still haggling the fare. She considered joining him, to avoid having to decide how best to cope with her situation, but it'd ruin Raza's fun and for what? Because she was squeamish?

She considered the beggar anew, and decided he was as harmless as the big man in the alleyway had proven to be, last night. She couldn't know how this man came to be the way he was, and when she thought about it, it didn't matter. Wasn't it enough he'd been reduced to getting about on a makeshift skateboard? She recalled the children at the airport, how Raza had said they were involuntarily part of a mafia operation.

The man kept his hand raised, but it was wavering. It must have been an effort to keep his hand upturned above head-height. Jasmine chose this alone as enough to warrant charity. The man struggled enough in his daily life, than be reduced to struggling for a couple of dollars. She wished she'd had a few more servings of Malika's goats' feet stew she could hand out.

Jasmine dived under her shirt to where her traveller's wallet was strapped to her body for safe-keeping. Nervous about inadvertently exposing her belly in public, she fumbled quickly with the zip and fished out a ten-thousand rupee note. It seemed excessive, but the exchange rate between dollar and rupee was crazy, so she didn't think twice, and handed the money over.

The man took it, mumbling again and bowing his head in deference to her, or so she thought until she heard him thanking his God, and not her. Jasmine didn't mind; charity was not for self-gratification, she reminded herself.

The man paused, studying the note, eyeing Jasmine through his dirty locks. Her eyes dropped to the money in his hand just as it disappeared into the folds of his clothes. A grin cracked the dirt of his face. Jasmine did a quick mental calculation and realised she'd just handed over the equivalent of a hundred dollars.

"Oh, wait..." she began, reaching out to the man, staying her hand as he scooted backwards, his rusty wheels grinding the concrete when they wouldn't turn. "I mean, wait, let me swap that for another one."

She knew it was futile, even if the man hadn't realised her error. How could she exchange a gift already given? She felt her cheeks get hot with embarrassment. All she could do was wish the man well, watching as he clawed his way down the path, glancing surreptitiously over his shoulder at her.

A chugging of a small engine close behind her announced the success of Raza's mission. She spun to see him directing the rickshaw-wallah to pull alongside the pole, and when he beckoned her to join him in the back of the rickshaw, the driver became visibly upset, arguing with Raza in Urdu. The debate was punctuated with English words and phrases, and she distinctly heard the man say "special foreign tax" whilst pointing at her.

"What are you talking about, *Baba?*" said Raza to the driver, shifting to English for Jasmine's benefit and giving her a sly smile. "Come on, let's drive. *Chelo.*"

The driver gestured for Raza to leave the vehicle.

"Foreigners don't weigh any more than locals, Baba," Raza snapped. "She is my wife, so don't insult me, brother. Let's go, stop whining."

Raza held the rear flap open for Jasmine to climb inside, and as the rickshaw puttered along Lahore's streets, the driver glared at them via his rear-view mirror. Not even the sight of a forklift carrying a car above the traffic in front of them at a roundabout could distract the driver from contemplating the evident betrayal of his passengers in outwitting him in his extortion attempt. Jasmine, on the other hand, was gobsmacked by the sight.

"Pakistani towing service," grinned Raza. "That's how they tow illegally parked cars here."

"Don't even worry about the parking fine, the damage bill alone is a deterrent," laughed Jasmine.

Clearing the roundabout, they were steered alongside another rickshaw where immediately a conversation was struck between the rickshaw-wallahs. The other driver looked surprised, glancing back into the rickshaw at Jasmine and furrowing his brow.

"What are they saying?"

"He's warning the other driver," Raza said. "Watch out for the Paki-boy and the gora-woman, they're tricksters."

Jasmine fell against Raza, laughing, but by the time they reached their destination she'd taken pity on the driver and made sure to tip, though not nearly as generously as she had with the beggar. The rickshaw-wallah sniffed, stuffing the notes down his *kameez* and angling his little vehicle into the slipstream of traffic in one smooth motion. Their confidence with the crazy traffic never failed to impress Jasmine.

The distance between actual tarmac and the buildings was greater here, Jasmine noticed, whereas other parts of the city the roads had reached right up to the doorsteps of the businesses. Masses of people gathered here in a makeshift market, purchasing all manner of fruit and vegetable. Scooters and auto-rickshaws wound slowly between the shoppers, turning the bazaar into a meeting spot for drivers to convene and smoke together. Of the buildings, they were evidently even older than the rest of the city she'd seen. Not one looked as though it had been constructed in her lifetime, thought Jasmine.

"This is Mori Gate," Raza said, as though reading her thoughts. "It's one of old twelve gates to the Walled City."

"Well, the *old* part is definitely fitting," Jasmine said, wandering her eyes across the ancient architecture, marvelling when Raza informed her it was over a thousand years old.

"Come on, I'll show you where the actual gate used to be."

They stepped away from the main road and into the wide thoroughfare leading into the Walled City. Like the rest of Lahore, the Walled City didn't reach into the heavens like cities in most countries did; there was an understated beauty to the place, no building higher than four stories, and each stone edifice marred by lichen and cracks. Lined along the street leading to the entrance of the Walled City were over a dozen stalls full of fresh fish. The stench was overbearing, and a woman passing by with a shopping bag full of fish heads chuckled when Jasmine showed her disgust at the smell wafting from the bag.

"You certainly know how to show a girl a good time, Mr. Makhdoom," she joked.

"Mori Gate is famous for the fish market," Raza explained, plugging his nostrils with two fingers. "People come from all over to get their seafood here."

Other stalls included brand-new *tandoor* ovens, brass dishes polished to such a shine they looked almost gold, and a herd of small goats whose curly-hair had been dyed blue, red, or green. And everywhere was the noise of people, chattering, haggling, beeping horns for passage. It was a hive of activity, enough to make Jasmine's head spin. But she loved every moment of it, recalling the books and films of her youth, tales of magic lamps and intrepid explorers.

"This is amazing," gushed Jasmine. "It's like stepping into the past."

"This is nothing yet," Raza promised. "Wait until we get a lot further in. The daylight practically disappears in there."

Jasmine smiled at the prospect, idly reaching her fingers out to a fence of coloured string alongside their course. There were thick hanks of it looped along from picket to picket spiked into the sunbaked earth.

"Whoa," cried Raza, gently lifting her hand away from the string. "Careful there."

Jasmine was amused.

"Why, do you think it'll kill me?"

"No, but it might cut your fingers off," he said, and pointed down the line of string where two small boys in pale blue *shalwar-kameez,* one sporting a cap with Mickey Mouse ears atop, were dipping a paint-brush into a bowl. Brows knitted with keen concentration, they deftly applied their mix to the string. "It's *diamond dust.* They coat the string in glass shards to cut their competitor's kites out of the sky."

Jasmine bent over to get a closer look at the string, and saw it glinted under the sun. A fine layer of ground glass was dusted onto it.

"Wow, they take flying kites pretty seriously around here," she said, scoffing.

"Almost a national sport," nodded Raza.

The boys had noticed Jasmine's scrutiny, and grinned to themselves at being acknowledged by a foreigner. Jasmine waved to them and they excitedly waved back. The one wearing the mouse ears ran up to her and handed her the cap, before running back to join his companion with the dusting.

"He just gave me his hat," Jasmine said, perplexed.

"It's an honour to meet you, that's why," smiled Raza. "It's probably his most prized possession, besides the kites. People like to show their appreciation with grand gestures here."

Jasmine tried the hat on, feeling awkward about accepting something so meaningful to someone with so little, but when she saw the boy beaming proudly, she understood. He would now be the talk of the neighbourhood for quite some time to come, because a foreigner had accepted his gift. She felt silly wearing the mouse ears, but the twinkle in the boy's eyes more than made up for it.

"Come," said Raza, intertwining his fingers with hers despite the stern disapprovals from passersby. "I want to show you something else."

Raza steered Jasmine toward a stall decorated with woollen tassels and dyed cloth. A variety of fish were on display, but no-one approached to inspect the wares. The tall man behind the stall had an aloof disposition, with a prophet's beard and kohl-rimmed eyes. A hand-painted sign told them he was Kamboo the Najumi.

"Salam, fish-wallah," greeted Raza with a little laugh.

"Salam," the man returned tiredly, doubtless having heard the gag a hundred times. "Fortune, yes?"

Raza nodded, looking to Jasmine.

"Pick your fish," Kamboo said, addressing her

directly.

"Okay," she mused, pouting her bottom lip in thought as she perused the carcasses, a golden scaled one the length of her arm finally catching her eye. "How about that one?"

"Mahseer, good choice, first class," the *najumi* said, winking at her as he swung the fish by the tail onto his chopping board.

"Oh, but that'll be too much for us and your grandmother," said Jasmine, turning to Raza, hoping he'd intercede on her behalf. In truth, she saw how dirty the board was, stained with the remnants of other fish, but in front of the vendor she couldn't confess how unhygienic she found it.

Raza grinned. "It's not for eating. Watch."

Kamboo took her selection and sliced the length of its belly with a rusted blade. Its guts spilled out across his chopping board, steaming in the air. The man wasted not a moment, plunging his hands inside the opening and rummaging around.

"What on Earth is he doing?" Asked Jasmine sceptically.

"He's a fortune teller, a *najumi*," said Raza.

Kamboo yanked the remaining innards free with a wet, sucking sound. He spread the entrails evenly across his board, looping them between his fingers as he went, lifting the entire mass into the air to form a slimy web, reminding Jasmine of the string game cat's-cradle she played as a child.

"Now he's divining," Raza said quietly, entranced by the *najumi's* manoeuvres with the fish entrails. "Fish-guts divination. Some use tarot cards, some use green parrots and a deck of cards."

"This is definitely one of the weirder ones," said

Jasmine.

The man peered closely at the configuration he'd created, slowly rotating his hands and deftly catching the loops of intestine with his pinkie or index as they slipped free of the tangle.

"This big news," he mumbled thoughtfully. "Very big news."

On Raza's dare, Jasmine asked the *najumi* what her fortune was.

"Danger and disaster," he disclosed in heavy tones, adding something in Urdu that Jasmine didn't understand. In broken English he continued: "You will big sacrifice, very much suffer. The brightest star become the most dark. You should leave Pakistan, now."

"What the hell kind of a fortune is that, you bastard motherless goat?" raged Raza.

A small crowd had gathered behind the couple to watch the fortune unravel, and those in the bazaar who hadn't stopped from curiosity at the white lady (accompanied by one of their own, no less!), now stopped to stare at Raza's outburst. Though not rare, public displays of emotion were uncommon, nonetheless, and the people were amused by his sudden temper. All but the *najumi* himself, who tugged at his earlobes apologetically, sputtering apologies in Urdu.

"Yeah, I'll make you sorry..." growled Raza.

Jasmine pulled on Raza's arm, alarmed by his anger and worried about the crowd at their back.

"Just leave it, babe," she implored. "It's just some stupid fun, anyway."

"Nah, fun would've been something different, not going on about death and stuff," Raza snorted, allowing himself to be led away. "What a thing to say, and to a foreigner!"

His words annoyed Jasmine.

"Why should I be treated any differently, Raza? I thought it was rather refreshing to hear something a bit different, even if it's a load of bull."

"I'm afraid that's all we might get around here: a load of bull."

"At least it's not pork," said Jasmine, trying for levity.

She grinned at him cheekily, poking him discreetly in the ribs. Reluctantly he gave her a lopsided smile to acknowledge the joke.

"Good, now that you're in a better mood, you can explain to me this new world we're entering."

"Oh, it's a new world alright," said Raza, warming again to his role as tour-guide. "There's nothing like the Walled City to take you back in time."

As they made their way deeper, the buildings either side closed over, their eves touching until there was no daylight visible. Strings of light bulbs lit the thoroughfares and every fifty paces or so the lane would branch into two, sometimes three, snaking away into dimly-lit passages filled with all manner of goods. Presently, they found themselves in the linen section of the old city, piles of folded blankets reaching to the ceiling and canopies above, tottering as Raza led a gobsmacked Jasmine deeper into the increasingly narrowing spaces.

"*A whole new world,*" Raza sang softly, and Jasmine could see him smiling at his own joke.

CHAPTER 6

The rocky cavern, lit seemingly by ethereal means, was quite large. To its inhabitants, it was known as the Elucidation Chamber, and they had adorned the walls with crudely carved arcane symbology. Similarly, the floor had been scored, though the large concentric rings reaching out to the walls had a more practical employ. Water had been released into their channels, until all the rings were filled to the brim. Six positions on the outer ring were marked by a seal, and upon each stood creatures with bestial features. These were the Jamallans, a sect of chuwa, creatures neither human nor rat, but a mutual fusion. Aligned with each creature, and positioned on an inner ring, was a stalactite with blue flame issuing from their tips. At the very centre of the concentric rings was a raised brick dais, the integrity of the structure beginning to crumble in places from age. The entire tableau was as of a labyrinth. The centre dais was flat on top, and inscribed thereon a symbol, resembling a standing fish with a circumflex accent above. The Jamallans called this *Mai-m-Mîn*, or the Dark Star.

The room resounded with a low chant the Jamallans had taken up, their voices comingling to create a unified mantra, each chuwa falling into synch with the next until their mantra vibrated the very air in the room.

The water welling in the grooves on the floor began to stir. First, it was subtle, but by means of prolonged chanting the water began to roll on itself, defying its own nature to converge inwards and upwards.

The tallest of the six, Kha'i, felt pleased by the outcome. The mantra was especially important, he believed, for the group to maintain a modal quality, a state of vibration wherein all energy defying their achievements would be released. It had long been a source of transcendence for the chuwa. That the water – and it was ordinary water by all accounts – had responded so lively to the tremor of their mantra proved his course was clear. There were some amongst his species who were of the opinion Kha'i and his community of Jamallans were misguided. He knew otherwise.

A shadow appeared in an archway.

The chanting ceased so suddenly it was as though all sound in the Elucidation Chamber had been sucked out in a vacuum. Strange how it only echoed when their voices were in full flight.

Kha'i motioned the shadow forward, his fierce eyes following the movements of the newcomer as it crossed the chamber. As was custom, only certain individuals were allowed to enter the Elucidation Chamber exposed to its raw energy, so the chuwa who now approached wore a clay mask, fashioned to be indistinctly anthropomorphic. In its taloned hands

it carried a baby, its soft brown skin dusted with the soil of the corridors beyond the chamber. The baby was passed across to Kha'i, and seeing the monster that glowered down at it, the baby instantly launched into a wail. Kha'i sniffed contemptuously.

"What news, then?"

The chuwa who had relinquished the baby rubbed its hands together fretfully.

"The Jilted Bride of Darkness was most pleased with our offering, thankfully."

"Of course," said Khai tiredly. "And?"

"A couple have come," the chuwa said. "A man, with a woman. He will be marked, and she will have hair from the sun."

All the chuwa in the room turned to stare at the masked messenger.

"From the sun?" Kha'i repeated slowly, arching a brow.

"She brings death and destruction." The chuwa looked around the room, its eyes glistening through the holes in the mask. "That's... that's what the Bride said, at least."

Kha'i slapped the chuwa across the head, dislodging the mask. Beneath the blow, it was Pirak who cowered, the hairless patch of white skin on the side of his face wrinkling in fear of Kha'i. The congregation gasped, for Pirak's vitiligo condition was considered a sign of weakness, since the vibration mantra was also considered to improve melanin within the chuwa. Pirak had long since been deemed unworthy by those granted access to the Elucidation Chamber.

"Cover your shame," hissed Kha'i.

Pirak offered his apologies, scrambling to put his

mask back in place.

"So, a marked man," mused Kha'i thoughtfully, turning his back on the disgraced Pirak. "We will have him back in our fold. We will need him."

Pirak understood there was no further need of his presence, and slunk from the room with his head lowered, not in reverence but from refutation.

The chuwa nodded solemnly at one another, murmuring amongst themselves as Kha'i cradled the baby on the top of the dais, covering the emblem inscribed thereon. The baby had ceased its cries, staring up at Kha'i miserably, pouting its bottom lip.

"Now, now, child, let's turn that frown upside down," said Kha'i, raising his arm in the air and extending his claws, before bringing it down in a lethal swipe.

CHAPTER 7

After an hour idly wandering the dimly lit passageways of the Walled City, Raza and Jasmine emerged from the other side onto Shahi Mohallah Street, headed toward the grand Badshahi Mosque. The spires and domes of the mosque could be seen rising behind the buildings that lined the street ahead. A gaggle of painted girls passed, eyeing Raza and giggling amongst themselves at the Mickey Mouse ears Jasmine wore. She noted they didn't wear their *dupattas* over their heads like most women, choosing to drape them loosely over their shoulders. The girls continued boisterously along a street to Jasmine's left, taunting men as they went.

"Who on Earth are they?" Jasmine said, staring after them. Their brazenness fascinated her.

"Prostitutes," said Raza. "That's the famous Shahi Mohallah up there, otherwise known as Hira Mandi. It's Lahore's red-light district."

Jasmine pulled her head back and gave Raza a funny look.

He put his hands up in surrender. "Hey, never was a patron so don't look at me like that."

"Not that, stupid," Jasmine laughed. "I mean, I didn't think there'd be brothels here. Isn't it banned?"

"Lots of things are," smirked Raza. "But Hira

Mandi's an institution. Besides, it's all mafia controlled now, and corruption keeps the whole thing going. Gone are the days when it was governed by women alone, out to make an honest living."

"Men just fuck everything up," Jasmine said, shaking her head and watching as the girls went around the bend further into Shahi Mohallah.

"This is where a lot of artists live, too," Raza said. "It's not obvious, but there's a sort of bohemia to this area, I suppose."

"The city of your birth never ceases to amaze," Jasmine said. "And so close to a mosque!"

"Not sure if you noticed," Raza said, "but we passed about six mosques inside the Walled City."

Jasmine stared wide-eyed at him.

"It's true," laughed Raza, leading her along Shahi Mohallah Street and through the huge wooden doors to the gardens in front of the huge mosque.

This was definitely a tourist-driven area, with buses lined on the street opposite the gardens to unload sightseers. To her right were the grounds of the impressive Fort, and to their left was the Badshahi Mosque. They spent the better part of the day exploring the battlements, and later the courtyard and surrounding arcades, carved from red sandstone and inlaid with white marble. Jasmine stood outside in the sun, watching Raza pray inside the central niche, beneath the largest of the mosque's domes. Locals watched her intently, as fascinated by her as she was by the grand architecture.

When Raza was finished, they returned to the quiet neighbourhood flanking the mosque where they bought some fried chicken from the renowned Cooco's Den to take home for dinner.

"Right, you remember the trick with the rickshaw?" Raza asked, handing Jasmine the bag of chicken to hold.

Jasmine nodded, so Raza crossed the street to haggle whilst Jasmine turned back to the shops and pretended to peruse the delicacies on display. She was meandering slowly from one stall to the next, away from Cooco's Den, when the sound of a raised voice further along caught her attention. It came from a sliver of an alleyway, and it hadn't gone unnoticed that the locals were deliberately keeping their distance from it. Jasmine cautiously approached the entrance to the alley, and peered around the corner. Down the lane she saw a man and a woman arguing. No, she saw a man yelling at a woman. Jasmine realised the woman was desperately poor, her clothes barely rags. Of the man, he was the woman's direct opposite, bedecked in finery and gold rings flashing on his fingers.

The man's hand swung through the air and slapped the woman across the face.

Jasmine let out an audible gasp, her breath catching in her throat. She hadn't expected the slap, though judging by the way the poor woman simply bowed her head in response, Jasmine supposed the woman had. The man backhanded the woman across the face a second time, berating her.

"Whoa!" yelled Jasmine, instinctively. "Stop it!"

There was a moment when all the players in the tableau froze, as though the stage lights had unexpectedly come up mid-performance. The man turned his head slowly in Jasmine's direction, his eyes bulging insanely. Jasmine's blood throbbed in her temple, and her mouth felt dry.

As if for Jasmine's benefit alone, the man turned upon his victim and growled in English: "Be more pathetic, you dried up old womb. Look more distraught. Earn your keep, you dog."

His words wormed their way through Jasmine's mind, and without meaning to she stepped forward into the alleyway and called out to the man again.

"Ahmad, please..." whimpered the beggar-woman pitifully, perhaps adopting English simply because she'd been reprimanded in it, and assumed it the new standard.

Whatever the reason, the hate in the man's eyes was enflamed, and he curled his hand into a fist, striking the woman on the jaw so hard she fell to her knees in the dirt with a pitiful cry.

"NO!" screamed Jasmine, dropping the bag of chicken to the ground. "Hands off, you prick!"

She was storming into the alleyway now, her body rigid with a mix of anger and fear, the adrenalin coursing through her body, making her feel lean and dangerous.

"What do you want, you white slut?"

The man's eyes had narrowed to slits. He turned to face her.

"Leave her alone!" What had the beggar-woman called him? "Ahmad. Leave her alone, or I'll call the police."

The man laughed mean-spiritedly. It was the mirth of a man holding all the cards, emboldened by arrogance and might.

"Piss off, *goree*. Police have no power here. You want to call for anybody, you call for me."

"Jasmine!"

It was Raza, who had appeared at the entrance of

the alleyway, the spilled bag of chicken at his feet. Behind him, in the hazy sunshine of a Lahori afternoon, was a rickshaw. He sprinted down to Jasmine and took her by the arm.

"So sorry about this, Hajji," he stuttered to Ahmad. "We're just ignorant tourists. Please forgive us. She doesn't know any better."

"I do know better," Jasmine countered angrily.

"She's a fiery one, your little bitch," smirked Ahmad. "Ever want to sell her, let us know."

Jasmine ground her teeth, staring hard at Ahmad. But Raza simply grimaced and nodded, hoping to humour the man.

"Leave it alone, I'm serious," he whispered into Jasmine's ear as she looked pitifully down at the beggar-woman.

Realising his wife might press the issue further, Raza wrapped his arms about her waist and hoisted her off her feet, attempting to carry her back to the entrance of the alleyway. She put up a fight, struggling in his arms, trying to wrest free, the mouse ears falling from her head to the ground and landing in a puddle of mud and donkey piss. Raza's shirt rode up his torso in the effort, his bulging scars running across his belly exposed for Ahmad to see. The man's eyes widened with recognition.

"How dare you!" spat Jasmine when Raza let her go out on the street. "That woman needs our help!"

Raza's face hardened.

"Come on, I've got a rickshaw, let's go."

"No, damn you. You can go, but I'm staying to–"

Raza, exasperated, turned on her and shook her by the shoulders.

"Shut up! Just listen, okay? That man? He's mafia.

A gangster. I know a woman's in trouble, Jasmine, but we could both be in a lot of trouble, maybe even dead, if we interfere."

Jasmine had never seen Raza so afraid before. Not in all their adventures together facing the dangers of rock-climbing, or base-jumping, had her husband ever flinched at the near-misses or the falls. But now his eyes held genuine fear, and Jasmine was stunned by it.

"Let's go."

Raza's final appeal. She understood it as an instruction, filled with consequence. Not for her, but them both. Raza wasn't a man prone to flights of fancy, so if he said Ahmad posed a genuine threat to them, then she believed it.

As she climbed into the back of the auto-rickshaw, the driver began to protest, insisting on a foreigner tax to the fare, but Raza, readying himself to follow behind Jasmine, ordered the man to shut his mouth and drive.

As Raza's foot mounted the step a gun was pressed to his temple. He paused, his hands gripping the handles of the rickshaw.

"Out."

Raza did as he was told, and backed slowly away from the auto-rickshaw. Ahmad stood beside him, holding the gun, ordering Raza to his knees. Knowing better than to argue, Raza lowered himself to the ground, his hands trembling with fear. The gun pressed again to the back of his skull, pushing his head down further.

"Please, I'm sorry," Jasmine said, peering out through the rear flap of the rickshaw.

The gangster wasn't interested in her appeals for

mercy.

"The scars on your belly," said Ahmad in considered tones. "Why do you have them?"

"I don't know what you mean," replied Raza.

"Answer me, or I blow your brains out."

Raza's hands slapped on the road for support as he was pushed forward by the muzzle of the gun.

"I got them... I got them when I was a baby. Rolled too close to a fan."

Jasmine watched this interrogation from the rear of the rickshaw. She glanced about the street, hoping someone might help, but the street was mysteriously deserted. The influence this man and his so-called mafia connections had was apparent. They were in real danger.

Ahmad scoffed at Raza's explanation for the scars.

"You're coming with me," he decided.

"No, please," pleaded Jasmine.

Whatever happened here, she knew Raza couldn't be taken. It might be the last he'd be heard from again.

"Go home, babe," gasped Raza, tears dropping from his nose into the dry dust on the road.

"She's coming, too," Ahmad said. "Get out of the rickshaw."

"No, please, just me," said Raza.

The gun tapped the back of his skull several times. "Shut up."

Jasmine gingerly crawled from the rear of the rickshaw, fighting the urge to kneel beside her husband and hold him, to shield him from this brute's violence. Ahmad looked her up and down slyly, a lascivious smile showing yellowed teeth and receding gums.

"And you," he said, clutching at a handful of her blonde hair and twining the locks about his fingers, "you'll work the brothels, as our star attraction."

The smile left his face just as a rock bounced off the back off his head. Like a tree felled, the gangster let go of Jasmine's hair and fell sideways, crashing into the dirt.

Shocked, Jasmine looked from the fallen man to the alleyway across the street. The beggar-woman stood there, stoic, seemingly all fear gone from her, though Jasmine could faintly see the woman's entire body shaking with either fear or adrenalin. She looked not back at Jasmine, though, but at where Ahmad lay on the ground at Jasmine's feet. In the woman's face there was resignation: she knew it was a suicidal move. When their eyes finally met, the two women nodded at one another in silent gratitude.

"Run!"

Raza had found voice, and was bundling Jasmine into the rear of the rickshaw. Panic-stricken, the driver beseeched them to seek the service of another rickshaw-wallah.

"Drive, you idiot!" barked Raza, and shoved a one-thousand rupee note into the man's hands.

The driver inspected the note against the light, and satisfied, started the engine just as Ahmad rose to his feet with murder in his eyes. The rickshaw pulled away in a puff of blue smoke as the gangster retrieved his gun from the road. Jasmine watched through a tear in the vinyl behind her head, expecting him to fire on the rickshaw, but instead the man turned to the beggar-woman and took aim.

"No," whispered Jasmine, horrified. Then loudly: "Turn around. Turn the rickshaw around!"

The crack of the gun coincided with the beggar-woman's body crumpling to the ground. The gangster was staring straight at the rickshaw when the fatal shot rang out, and Jasmine could feel the man's hatred boring into her. She faced the front, gasping and sweating.

"Fuck..."

Raza squeezed her arm.

"It's not your fault," he said quietly. "You didn't know."

Time became irrelevant, suddenly. She didn't know if only seconds had passed, or if an hour, but when Jasmine finally found voice it was dry and croaky, filled with anger.

"Not my fault? Not my fault?"

"What?" Raza's voice sounded small, as if the leftover of a half-remembered dream.

"What the hell do you mean by that?"

"Calm down, baby..."

"No, you calm down!" she snapped. "Don't call me baby! I'm not a fucking child."

"Jasmine, you're in shock. It's okay."

The rickshaw-wallah's eyes in the mirror, watching her fearfully. Why? She didn't have a gun. It wasn't her that was armed.

"He had a gun, Raza!"

Raza's jaw was clenching.

"Okay, just hold on, we'll get out of this."

Jasmine faced him for the first time since they'd escaped. He was afraid, she saw, but he was also determined. He would set things right, somehow, that she knew. That was what she felt when she looked into his eyes now. Raza, the protector.

"Promise," he said evenly.

The driver said something in Urdu, and Raza opened the side flap to peer behind them. Jasmine craned her neck to peer through the tear, and saw amongst the insanity of the Lahori traffic there was one particular auto-rickshaw with an absurd sunflower painted on the front fender zig-zagging between all other vehicles at excessive speed.

"He's following us," Jasmine said, terror strangling her voice.

Raza instructed the driver to increase the speed, but the man struggled to control the vehicle under intense pressure, and soon Ahmad's rickshaw had closed the distance. Through the tear Jasmine could see the gangster had commandeered the rickshaw himself, and she hoped another life hadn't been taken as a result of her interference. The whites of Ahmad's eyes shone brightly through the bug-spattered windshield of his rickshaw. Never had Jasmine felt such gripping fear as she did now. It held her heart and squeezed.

"Just breathe, breathe, honey," Raza was yelling at her, his face in hers. "You need to control your breathing."

She was slouched in the seat. Was she having a heart attack? Her body felt like it was betraying her. Over her husband's shoulder gangster's rickshaw idled alongside. She tried to warn Raza of the threat at his back, but struggled to make the words form.

"Jasmine! Jasmine!"

The panic in his voice told Jasmine there was something seriously wrong with her. But it was he who was in danger.

The rickshaws collided, their driver cursing as they were steered off-course, a bus horn blaring long and loud to her left. Raza yelling; shots fired. Then the sudden impact of a crash, their bodies flung like rag-dolls toward the windshield.

Silence.

Or what Jasmine thought was silence. Her ears popped, and the sound of chaos followed.

People were shouting outside, traffic banking up behind, sounding horns in frustration. The rickshaw driver bellowing, his legs crushed beneath the dislodged seat. And Raza's voice, demanding again, barking orders.

"Out! We need to get out!"

Jasmine's mind snaps into clarity, as though she'd been sinking in murky water the entire time and only now had resurfaced. She looks about at the carnage. The rickshaw was wrecked. Their auto-rickshaw had run head-on into a wooden cart laden with massive bales of fabric. It had cushioned the impact, or else they'd all be dead. Through the smashed windscreen she could see Ahmad's rickshaw, stopped in the traffic yond the wooden cart. She didn't need to Raza to tell her that the gangster would be upon them any moment now; she could see the madman shoving his way past the motorcyclists and donkeys to reach them.

She felt her legs. They worked. Her breathing had returned to normal. She flung aside the flap on the rickshaw and stumbled out into the street, his hands on her shoulders to let her know he was right behind her. The driver would have to fend for himself, although we neither of them there it was unlikely the gangster would bother with him. It was they he wanted, and he wouldn't waste a moment in pursuit.

"This way," said Raza, pointing own the road.

They fought their way through the gathering crowd, slapping at any who tried to bar their path. Glancing over her shoulder, Jasmine could see the gangster doing likewise. In a fury, he raised the gun in the air and fired, scattering the people. He now had a clear line of fire directly at Raza's back.

Jasmine wrapped her arm around Raza's and pulled him into a shop, ignoring the questions from the shop-keeper about their welfare. They raced through to the rear before realising there was no exit. Buildings here weren't designed like they were in Australia, Jasmine realised.

"The window," said Raza, and as they climbed through it they could hear Ahmad demanding of the proprietors as to their whereabouts.

They found themselves in a narrow space between buildings, almost too narrow for Raza to fit. He stood on tip-toes as they inched their way along, away from the melee of the road they'd crashed on. At the other end was the glimpse of a quieter street. Fewer witnesses to direct the gangster as to their direction.

Though it didn't seem to matter now, for a hissing sound alerted them to Ahmad's discovery of their escape route. Jasmine could see the gangster had poked his head out the window, and was watching them. Then he ducked back in, and Jasmine wondered if he intended to continue the pursuit or finally give it up.

"He's asking the shop-wallahs for another way behind the building," said Raza, as though reading her thoughts.

Jasmine's heart sank. If the gangster found his way to the street ahead before they could, they were as good as dead, or worse. Ahmad had promised a life of captivity in a brothel, the thought of which made Jasmine's blood run cold. She'd kill herself before that would happen.

She trod on something soft, and heard squeaking by way of protest. Something furry and wet brushed her ankle.

"Rats," she murmured.

"Don't let them bite you, they're diseased," Raza warned.

"And how exactly do I do that?" said Jasmine, exasperated.

"They hate ammonia, and we're dehydrated," said Raza.

Only now could she smell the sharp sting of urine.

"Did you just piss yourself?" she asked incredulously.

He grunted by way of reply. Jasmine considered following his advice, but the street was closer by the moment, and her bladder wouldn't budge anyway, so fearful was she that in any second Ahmad's face would swiftly appear in the gap ahead.

She broke free of the space, nearly falling on her face in her desperation to be away from the rats scurrying around her feet. Raza stumbled after her, quickly taking stock of their surroundings.

"Residential neighbourhood," he said, ignoring the bemused expressions of the few people leaning from balconies, watching them as he got his bearings.

He needn't have bothered, for Ahmad appeared at one end of the street, gun in hand. He stood for a few heartbeats, considering them, before taking up the chase again.

"Go!"

Jasmine didn't need Raza's encouragement on that

score. She was already taking flight, uncertain where she was headed but content only to be headed away from the imminent threat. The street ahead dog-legged several times, plain concrete buildings towering either side, the smog-blotted sky beyond still bright with the day. Eventually they staggered onto a wide main road.

"Do you know where we are?" Jasmine asked between breaths.

"No clue," admitted Raza.

He looked around for a means of escape, and saw the young men gathered around their scooters and considered trying to steal one, but knew he was outnumbered. Then he saw the forklift readying itself before a car nearby. The street sign was marked as a no parking zone.

"This way," Raza said, taking Jasmine by the hand and racing toward the forklift.

Making sure the mast of the forklift blocked their view of the driver, and thus, his of them, Raza yanked open the rear door on the offending car and ushered Jasmine inside. When he'd followed and carefully closed the door behind him, Jasmine looked bewilderingly at him.

"Head down," he said, just as Ahmad broke cover from the street they'd exited.

The forklift's tines scraped beneath the vehicle, jolting them.

Ahmad kept his head down, his arms crossed over Jasmine's back, praying his plan would work. As far as he could tell, the gangster hadn't seen them inside the car, and as long as the people on the street who'd witnessed them climb inside kept their mouths shut, all would go well.

Ahmad was shouting, insisting to be told their whereabouts.

The car jolted again as the tines began to lift. The whir of the hydraulics masked the gangster's demands. The forklift stopped lifting, the car rocking gently on the raised tines. There were voices outside. Raza and Jasmine held their breath.

The engine of the forklift revved once, and the hydraulics strained.

"No," whispered Raza, defeat underscoring his tone.

The motion Jasmine felt was not of dropping, but of swinging. She opened her eyes and peered up at the window, watching as the buildings slid from view.

"Raza..."

Raza glanced up, just as the swinging motion finished, to be replaced by a forward motion. He raised his head a little higher, just enough to peek over the door and see that they were in motion.

Relief washed over him, and he collapsed across the seat, nearly laughing in triumph.

The forklift had the car high in the air, ferrying it through the streets of Lahore for illegal parking, unwittingly carrying Raza and Jasmine to safety, away from Ahmad's reach.

"Fuck that guy," said Raza quietly.

Jasmine sat staring at the floor, and when he heard her sobbing uncontrollably, Raza let his fingers gently comb her hair.

Eventually the forklift came to a halt, lowering the vehicle to the ground. The tines fell away from the chasis with a crunch of metal and crushed exhaust pipes. Raza flung open the door, and he and Jasmine lurched out into the impound yard to the astonishment of the forklift operator, who began firing a dozen questions at them.

Raza shrugged at the man, running toward the row of shipping containers serving as the impound yard's barrier, slipping between them and out onto the street. Jasmine was right behind him, and this time when they sought the services of a rickshaw they didn't play their hiding game, but instead paid the full fare – "foreigner's tax" and all – directing the driver to make straight for Malika's home, and not to stop for anyone, no matter how maniacal they might appear.

This last instruction amused the rickshaw-wallah no end, but for Raza and Jasmine there was no mirth to be had. They sat tense the entire trip, flinching when a rickshaw or truck would backfire, nervous when they idled at intersections or in traffic jams.

By nightfall they had arrived back at Raza's grandmother's house, where the pair fled up the stairs to their room before they could be intercepted by the old woman. Right now, they wanted solitude and a warm blanket for the feeling of shock. An off-hand remark mumbled by Raza immediately brought Jasmine's underlying anger to the surface once more, however.

"Lucky escape? Raza, we were almost killed!"

Raza ignored her, running his hands through his hair repeatedly to rub the stress away. He only turned around when he heard her sobbing heavily. She was perched on the edge of the bed, her shoulders jerking violently. He sat gingerly beside her, rubbing her back to soothe her.

"I just want to go home," she sniffed. "Can't we do

that?"

"Sure, as soon as we can. I'll call the airline tomorrow and bring our flights forward."

"Good."

"Until then, we'll keep a low profile. I'll cancel the *walima* reception. The extended family will just have to come see us in Australia."

The news warmed Jasmine, for she knew how important it was to Raza's family to meet her, especially since she'd already come half-way across the world for it to happen. It was no small matter to simply cancel and up and leave again. But she wanted nothing more at this moment.

"They won't find us, will they? The gangsters?"

"No, babe," Raza assured her, shaking his head. "Look, I won't lie to you, people here have their ways. They can be very resourceful. But there's also a huge amount of people living in Lahore. It'd take them too long to find us, even if they're looking."

"You think they are?"

"I doubt it. They know they can bribe the cops to look the other way if we report it."

Jasmine shivered at the idea of a murder being so trivial.

"But the scar on your stomach," Jasmine ventured anxiously. "Why was he so interested in it?"

"I'm not sure."

Raza stared into space, unable to comprehend why the pale lines of scarred flesh across his belly could be of significance to anyone, and feeling fatigued by the day's events, he let out a huge yawn.

Outside their door, standing silently in the darkness of the landing, was Malika, listening intently to every word with a brooding expression.

CHAPTER 8

The room was dimly lit, and comfortably furnished. As befit the *badmash* – otherwise known as the mafia – Lakar Baga, the eponymous head of the Lakar Baga Badmash, sat reclined in a synthetic-leather chair, his pudgy fingers pressing out the creases in the fabric stretched across his bulging belly. They'd not long since eaten, the plate on the desk before him littered with the remnants of a chicken *biriyani*. It was his custom to nap for a short spell after eating, and the other men who occupied the room were so well versed in their roles that they'd all quietly played on their phones until their boss had awoken.

Goondas were what these men were. Simply put: gangsters. They knew their trade well, managing to climb the ranks to the favoured position of being able to partake in a *biriyani* with the boss and remain in the room while he slept. They each had skills which had helped elevate them to their current glories, and there were few in the complex organisation the *badmash* oversaw who would not strive for excellence, and thus ingratiate themselves to the private company of the big man himself.

So it was perplexing to all gathered when Ahmad, a lowly but ambitious *goonda* who had begun showing promise, was brought before them to explain he'd found a fully-grown man with peculiar – yet, distinctive – marks across his stomach.

"And you lost them?"

Lakar Baga's voice betrayed no emotion, but every man in the room felt the subtle shift in the air, as though a lightning storm had begun to gather unseen, the electricity it generated throbbing through the floor and walls.

"It was only by a slim chance that they escaped," Ahmad said, tripping slightly on his words and silently cursing himself for it. "Fate was against me in the matter."

Lakar Baga leaned forward, arching his brows, accompanied by a squeak as the chair protested beneath his weight.

"Don't bring fate into it, Ahmad. It has served me well throughout my life, and I won't hear a word against it."

Ahmad looked around the room at the other *goondas*, wondering if the talk of slighting fate was a joke. Seeing the impassive faces staring back at him, he decided it wasn't, and returned his attention back to the big boss, swallowing hard. His gulp was the only sound in the room.

"Yes, Baga *saab*, sorry," Ahmad stuttered.

The room tittered. Ahmad's faux-pas would make for choice slander once he was dismissed, that much was certain.

"This is just an educated guess, Ahmad – but then I *am* an educated man, so such speculation shouldn't be beneath me – but I would assume that this man with the rat-people's mark on him wouldn't be the only thing of interest to our future business partners, the chuwa?"

Lakar Baga scratched his belly, assuming an air of contemplation. Ahmad was clueless as to the big man's inference, but the room was not, or at least one of their number was not.

"*Saab*, you think the woman is, too?"

Ahmad knitted his brows at his peer's deduction. What would the chuwa, those damned rat-faced tunnel-dwellers, want with a *goree*?

"Yes, I do," said Lakar Baga, delighting in the surprise on Ahmad's face. "I think the rat-people might have been hoping for this, somehow. Otherwise, how does a man who is marked escape the attention of such creatures for... how old would you say the man was, Ahmad?"

Ahmad scratched his scalp. "Maybe close to thirty."

The *goondas* whistled in appreciation of their boss's cunning.

"You see, gentlemen? Nearly thirty years this man has gone undetected. Or been allowed to. Now he is here with this white woman. Imagine how business dealings with these rat-people, these *chuwa*, would be a whole lot more favourable if we had this couple in our possession."

The room, including Ahmad, nodded in agreement.

"Well, there it is, Ahmad," he continued, flavouring his tone with a note of finality. "It is now your task to bring me this foreign woman. That is all."

The big man looked away, distracted by a loose thread on his trouser leg. Ahmad turned to leave, incapable of making eye-contact with the other *goondas* in the room.

"And Ahmad..."

He stopped and turned, hoping for a token of gratitude from Lakar Baga for having brought what had turned out to be such valuable information.

"Yes boss?"

"Don't fuck it up, Ahmad, or I'll have your balls for my *biriyani*."

Ahmad swallowed hard, nodding submissively, and skulked from the lair of the Lakar Baga Badmash.

CHAPTER 9

When Raza's grandmother finally retired to her bedroom for the night, he and Jasmine crept down to the kitchen to make themselves hot tea and to snack on whatever they could find in the fridge. They'd been unable to face the old woman, at least for tonight, fearful any friendly prodding about their day might unleash a riot of detail from themselves. Neither wished to burden their host with their near-death experience.

Jasmine set the pot on the stove-top to boil the water while Raza went around checking to make certain all the doors and windows were locked. When he was inspecting his grandmother's wooden club, the one she used for thumping rats, he heard a scuffle beyond the front door, followed by a light rapping. He froze, straining to listen for more sounds, trying to discern who might be on the other side of the door.

"Please, just a little," came a small voice, definitely a child's, asking for alms.

A beggar.

"Sorry, not tonight," Raza called softly through the door, glancing back toward the kitchen to make sure his voice hadn't carried through to Jasmine. He didn't need her panicking about people at the door.

The child rapped on the door again, louder this

time. If this continued, Jasmine would surely hear. Raza pressed his palm flat against the door as he cracked it open, so it wouldn't squeak. He'd noticed earlier that the hinges needed oiling. Peering through the opening, he could see a small boy outside wearing only a grubby pair of shorts. The boy's hair was shoulder-length, his skin roughened by the elements. He held a palm up.

Raza sighed. He'd been brought up to observe the importance of *zakat*, the giving of alms. If he rejected the boy now, he flew in the face of his upbringing, and in his own grandmother's house, no less. He knew the neighbourhood would cast aspersions on Malika's character if her grandson were to be seen refusing a beggar.

The door was blessedly quiet as he opened it all the way. He dug into his pockets to search for a few rupee notes, smiling wistfully as the boy rubbed his little belly.

"Hungry, huh?" said Raza quietly.

The boy's fingers dug into the flesh of his belly, just below the bellybutton.

"Whoa, go easy on yourself there, little one," said Raza in mild alarm.

The boy merely smirked contemptuously at him, continuing to dig his fingers into the skin of his belly. Suddenly the skin split horizontally, the boy's whole hand slipping inside as if into a pouch.

"What the hell?"

Inside the wound the boy had created upon himself was a mass of squirming maggots. The boy's hand closed over them, and he yanked his hand free. For a horrifying moment Raza thought the boy intended to eat the larva, and stepped forward to stop him, eyes wide with disbelief.

It was a mistake. The boy opened his fist and from it flew a swarm of black flies, making for Raza's face. They latched themselves onto him, quickly crawling across his cheeks and eyelids, where they bored into the inner corner of Raza's eyes, scratching and crawling until they'd burrowed beneath his eyelids.

Raza screamed, thrashing about and clawing at his face. He could feel the flies, their hairy legs and stiff wings scratching at the soft underside of his lids, scraping over his eyeballs.

He could hear a ceramic mug smash in the kitchen as it was dropped to the floor, and Jasmine's alarmed voice calling out to him as she ran to his aid.

"The boy! He did something! I can't see!"

As Jasmine ran up beside Raza to take hold of his shoulders, she saw a dishevelled boy standing out on the street, backing slowly away. His eyes were like saucers, and she swore she saw him close a fatal wound on his belly as though it were never there.

"What did you do to him?" she screamed.

Shadows now, lengthening as they advanced down the street. Any neighbours or loiterers watching the scene unfold became agitated by the arrival of the newcomers, disappearing indoors or slinking down alleyways.

"Inside, Raza! This way!"

Jasmine tried to lead her husband to the safety of his grandmother's house, but he slipped on the ramp for scooters, falling heavily on the concrete and sliding down to the street. She half-expected the boy to laugh at her husband's misfortune, but he simply stared, as if intrigued by Raza's suffering.

The newcomers, cloaked in heavy robes with

hoods shadowing their faces, stopped before the boy. From their sleeve, one of the newcomers produced a small velvet purse, and handed it to the child. The purse wriggled, as though it contained a tiny creature, and from within came a squawk of displeasure.

"Your payment, as requested," the robed being said to the boy. "Be careful with it. It took us days to locate such a specimen in the Balouchistan desert, and for something long considered extinct, it's a rare treat you have."

The boy, for his part, looked disgruntled.

"What do I look like, an idiot?"

His voice, though a child's, seemed to Jasmine to be ancient. She couldn't quite tell why, and she didn't wish to know, either. She stared horrified at the exchange while she crept gingerly down the steps, reaching out for Raza.

Without another glance in her direction, the boy sauntered away, holding the purse up and flicking his finger against it, taunting the creature inside.

"Stay away from us," Jasmine warned the robed beings, having gotten Raza to his feet and up the stairs to the door.

She no sooner got him across the threshold and was slamming the heavy metal door closed when a hand shot out and stopped the door. It was a hairy hand, though the follicles appeared more like the fur of an animal. As did the nails, thick black claws curving off each finger.

Jasmine gasped, stumbling back, affording the interlopers the chance to advance inside and close the door behind them.

"Look, I'm sorry," Jasmine started, "I didn't know

you were mafia. Please, I won't tell anyone. Just leave us alone, please."

"We are not mafia," said one of the intruders, spitting the word out contemptuously. "We are chuwa."

"Show us the mark," said another, in a low rumble.

Jasmine looked dumbfounded, shaking her head.

"The mark!" snapped the first being. Its voice was like a whip-crack, making Jasmine jump. "The seal! The scar!"

"What's going on?" Raza said, with a tremulous voice. "Jasmine?"

"The man is marked, is he not?"

Jasmine nodded.

"Show us."

Fear rooted Jasmine to the spot, and she couldn't move. One of the beings – the chuwa, they called themselves – rushed forward and took her by the hair, shaking her like a rag-doll. Jasmine squealed from pain, her hands instinctively going to her abuser's grasp. His wrists were sinewy and strong, covered in thick, coarse fur. She pulled her hands back in revulsion, noting Raza wasn't the only marked one in the room. Burned into her assailant's wrist was a brand, a three-pronged sigil:

"Leave her alone!" barked Raza.

"Or you'll do what?" one of the intruders teased.

Jasmine put her hands up in surrender, and was

released for her compliance.

"Okay, just don't hurt us," she said, and then to Raza: "Baby, hold still, okay?"

"I can't see, Jasmine," he whined, his hands over his eyes. "They blinded me."

She lifted Raza's shirt to reveal the scars running across his stomach.

"Is this what you want to see?"

One of the intruders flipped back its hood, and Jasmine stared in astonishment. The man's face was neither human nor animal, but somewhere in between. It was covered in a fine fur, and his snout was like a beasts', with long whiskers curling back over his cheeks. His top lip twitched as he stared fascinated at Raza's scars, revealing incisors thick enough to bite clean through her arm. The light from the kitchen reflected in his eyes, and she saw they were completely black. If she didn't know any better, Jasmine would guess she was faced with a rat, not a man.

Slowly the creature reached a hand out, his deadly claws extending from the tips of his fingers as if ready for injury. Jasmine held her breath, her eyes watering, as the creature, the chuwa, glided his claws a hair's breadth from her husband's stomach, following the lines of his scars. They matched the creature's claws perfectly.

Jasmine shook her head, discerning the implication.

"No, no," she said, pleadingly. "He's not with you. He's my husband."

"Let's go," the chuwa simply said.

The other intruders crowded around Raza, looping their arms with his and lifting his feet from the floor.

Raza cried out for Jasmine.

"No!" she begged. "I love him!"

She hadn't expected such creatures to readily understand, much less be moved by, such appeals, given she saw nothing of humanity in their faces. Perhaps it was less a petition than it was a warning. Jasmine rushed forward, pushing through their number and grabbing Raza by the hand, trying to pull him away. She didn't think it would be so easy, of course, so when one turned on her she lashed out, striking the beast on the jaw.

Her blow barely fazed it. She was backhanded away, blood trickling from her nose, fresh tears springing to her eyes.

"You can't take him!" she growled, her anger rising through her chest. She felt hot and dizzy.

Malika's club stood against the wall, so Jasmine snatched it up and brought it down on her assailant's head. The chuwa staggered beneath the blow, so Jasmine took advantage of the gap left behind Raza.

But the chuwa were fast, with animalistic reflexes.

She was shoved back with such force she saw the room spin. Instinctively, she reached out, her rock-climbing experiences guiding her hand to find purchase, staving her from a fatal fall. When she had steadied herself, she saw she was mere seconds from dashing her brains against a timber cabinet behind her.

The creatures had stopped to watch her, and it appeared they'd all held their breath, as though her safety was somehow imperative.

"You bastards," she snarled, ready to relaunch her defensive, but when she went to right herself she winced in pain.

Her ankle had sprained in her free-fall.

The chuwa hurried Raza across the threshold.

"No!"

Jasmine limped across the hallway for the door.

The creature who had backhanded her spun around, lowering its head and baring its teeth. The hood slipped back with the motion, so it appeared to Jasmine as though the beast emerged from a hideous foreskin, eyes bulging and incisors ready for the kill. One side of the chuwa's face was hairless, a large patch of albino flesh marring its head.

"Stay," the chuwa hissed.

When he leapt effortlessly down to the street in one bound, forgoing the steps altogether, Jasmine saw the rest of the contingent had bundled her husband onto a wooden cart. They all mounted it to hold him down, covering his mouth with their hideous hands.

Malika appeared behind Jasmine, clutching her shawl at her throat, watching the creatures hold her grandson down on the wooden cart. In her white-knuckled grip she held a cast-iron skillet. The chuwa with the pale vitiligo marking paused at the wheel of the cart, making eye-contact with her. It nodded at Malika, and then launched itself onto the back of the cart, taking up the reins.

Two camels were tethered to the cart, and at the chuwa's snap on the reigns, they trotted down the darkened street toward the main road.

Jasmine screamed and screamed for them to stop. Her ankle had swollen, and she'd only made it as far as the bottom of the steps when the creatures – with her kidnapped husband – turned the distant corner and disappeared.

Only now did Jasmine notice Malika standing at the doorway.

"Do something!" she yelled at the old woman.

Malika stared dreamily up the empty street. For a moment, Jasmine thought the old woman might actually be sleep-walking with her eyes open. Jasmine hobbled up the steps and shook Malika by the shoulders.

"You stupid woman! Wake up! Raza is kidnapped! Help us!"

Malika glared angrily at Jasmine, squaring her shoulders in defiance. She thrust the useless skillet into Jasmine's hands, and stormed back into the house, disappearing into the depths.

"Fuck this," growled Jasmine, and glanced around the street for signs of life.

A fruit cart sat against a wall, a tattered tarpaulin stretched over the abundant wares. Behind it she saw an auto-rickshaw, and remembering how the rickshaw-wallahs from yesterday were wont to sleep inside their vehicles, Jasmine limped across the street hoping for an occupant. She was not disappointed.

"Hey, wake up," she said, slapping the driver across the face.

He mumbled something unintelligible, and turned over in his sleep. His breath reeked of petroleum fumes. A drunk, passed out on homemade hooch. She slapped him again, harder, and this time the man was more responsive, sitting upright and cursing her in Urdu. He rubbed at the side of his face.

"We have to hurry!" said Jasmine, climbing into the rear of the rickshaw uninvited.

The driver shook his head, scowling at her.

Jasmine struggled to find the right words in the

man's own language.

"*Jaldi* to... um... to *bara* mosque. *Bara masjid?*"

She held her arms wide to indicate a significant size.

"Badshahi?"

"Yes! That's the one!" shouted Jasmine enthusiastically. "I need to go there."

The man mumbled in Urdu, checking his wristwatch.

Jasmine felt in her back pocket, and produced an Australian five dollar note, left there from the plane trip. She thrust it at the rickshaw-wallah, hoping it was enough incentive.

"Badshahi?" the man said again, and Jasmine nodded.

The engine started, and the rickshaw puttered down the street toward its destination. Jasmine couldn't appreciate the milestone of having commandeered her first rickshaw; her mind was set only on the task of rescuing Raza. Lahore was a massive city, brimming with people, half its streets unmapped. She had no idea who the creatures were who had taken her husband, but she was certain the gangster from the day before had a hand in it, and the only place she could think to look for the bastard was at Shahi Mohalla, behind the big mosque.

From a darkened window, Malika watched Jasmine leave in the rickshaw. The snap of a wire spring-trap resounding behind her elicited no reaction. Only when Malika heard the wheeze of the dying rat did she turn to watch its death throes inside the rat-catcher's trap in the far corner of the room. A coldness came over the old woman's eyes, and it would have chilled Jasmine had she been there to see it.

CHAPTER 10

By the time the morning sun broke over the domes of the grand Badshahi Mosque, Jasmine had spent half the night searching the district of the Shahi Mohalla, boldly wandering its streets and alleyways, peering into the shadowy spaces between buildings where only a child could shimmy. She even strolled several times unmolested through Hira Mandi, the infamous red-light district, where she was stared at by both the sex workers and their clientele. If any mafia had been present, she'd been unable to distinguish them from the men who sought the services of the ladies loitering in the *haveli* doorways. In one sense, she'd never felt more unsafe in her entire life, the events of the day before included; in another, she simply didn't care.

At some point she'd approached a circle of policemen who were smoking and laughing close to the entrance gates of the mosque, hoping news of Raza's kidnapping would spur them into action, make them scour the neighbourhood and turn out homes in search of her husband. Instead, they'd laughed at her, either not realising she was serious or feigning ignorance. She'd wanted to hit them, shame them into doing their job, but each man had an AK-47 slung over his shoulder, and their laughter was the lynch-mob's laughter. Jasmine had quickly realised the police would be about as dangerous as the gangster, if provoked, so she'd left them to cat-calling her and continued her search of the neighbourhood.

Her feet now ached, so she rested beneath a tree coated in dust. Everything that stayed put too long was coated in dust, she'd realised. There was no escaping it. Even the sun struggled with the smog on the horizon line, blazing like a hellfire behind the gossamer veil of pollution.

The *azhan*, the call to prayer, sounded across the city, starting with the melodic one coming from the Badshahi's minarets behind her, lifting the pigeons from their roosts in flocks that silhouetted against the brightening sky, to the tinny and feeble calls from the speakers scattered throughout the Walled City before her. With it came life, a steady stream of sleepy men, mostly barefoot and bare-chested, rubbing their eyes in bemusement at seeing a white woman sitting alone in the streets at such an early hour. Jasmine studied each man in turn, hoping to recognise either Ahmad the gangster or one of the creatures from last night.

But in very little time the streets had become deserted again, the men having disappeared into the Walled City or into the mosque behind her. The *azhan*, likewise, had ceased, replaced with a low intonation as the men singularly prayed behind the walls surrounding the mosque.

Besides a long-haired homeless man chewing his nails as he lay in the dirt by a puddle, the only activity came from across the street, at the same coffee establishment she and Raza had bought the fried chicken: Cooco's Den. It was a narrow building, crammed between its neighbours, standing several stories high and painted a lurid pink and blue colour.

From it approached an old man, carrying a tea-cup and saucer. He waggled his head at Jasmine, passing her the tea without a word, whence he shuffled back to the café and disappeared inside.

Jasmine sniffed at the tea tentatively, and deciding it was safe enough, pushed back the skin that had formed on top and sipped. It was good, warming her belly. The sugar relaxed her, and she fell into a half-sleep, her eyelids fluttering open at the sound of anyone passing.

Eventually the street came to life, and the doors to the mosque were thrown wide for the general public. She recalled something Raza's mother had said about life in Pakistan, how it's different than in Australia where people rose early for morning exercises or communal breakfast. Here, people were more inclined to start the day much later in the morning. With the hubbub of market life now picking up, Jasmine decided it was time to keep moving, search the neighbourhood again and see if she couldn't find the kidnappers.

She crossed the street and found the old man from earlier sitting comfortably in the shade of an awning outside the café.

"*Shukriya,*" she said tiredly, passing him the empty tea-cup and saucer.

"No problem," he replied in English, smiling warmly and waggling his head.

She hesitated, wandering how best to ask, and decided the direct approach was best.

"Listen, do you know about the mafia here?"

The man continued to smile, seemingly oblivious to the question.

"No?" she stared at the man, hoping for a note of

recognition, but with none forthcoming she thanked him again for the tea and wandered out into the sun to begin her search anew.

She only managed a dozen steps before she was intercepted by a man her own age, his arms festooned with wristwatches. They reached from his wrist to elbow on both arms.

"Hello, what is your good name?" he asked, jangling the watches to get her attention.

Jasmine ignored the man.

"Hello, American?" he persisted.

"Bas," Jasmine snapped.

The man's eyes lit up in delight.

"Ooh, you can speak Urdu, very nice."

"I said fuck off."

The man muttered as he stopped following her.

But he wasn't the only one who had taken a vested interest in her, she'd noticed. For some time she'd been aware another man was following her, one who preferred to keep his distance. It was the homeless man from nearby Cooco's Den, the one who had been lying on the ground biting his nails. She used the side mirrors on the rickshaws parked road-side to observe the man following her. The rickshaw-wallahs all called out to her, but she ignored them.

Jasmine casually strolled across the street and into a pop-up stall, again ignoring the attentions of the seller, and browsed a stack of folded *shalwar-kameez*. Surreptitiously she stole a quick glance at her stalker, who had naively approached the stall thinking her distracted. They made eye-contact and the man froze, his already small pupils contracting even further into pinpoints. His eyes were strange; golden in colour, but where she expected to see the whites of his eyes, they were black. This, and his oversized teeth, gave him a faintly bestial appearance. Not at all like the creatures who had taken Raza, but it was enough.

"Stop!"

The man was alarmed by Jasmine's demand, and stumbled back into the flow of pedestrian traffic on the street. He stood a full foot taller than anyone else, and struggled to blend in. Jasmine had no trouble following his progress through the crowd.

Realising she was closing the gap, the man panicked, breaking into a run, shoving pedestrians aside to put distance between he and Jasmine.

"Wait! Stop!"

Jasmine was ignored, so she sprinted after the man, dodging the crowd by goose-stepping between them, recalling her skills on the football field to navigate the masses.

Her target was nimble, however, and at one point he had ducked down close to the entrance to the Walled City, effectively disappearing. Realising she'd lost him, Jasmine stopped and took stock of the situation, exasperated by the crush of people. To pursue him into the narrow corridors of the Walled City would be a lost cause. They branched into too many thoroughfares. She ran her hands through her hair, turning in a circle as she let herself think.

Back the way she'd come, she noticed a head standing out above the rest. She saw his long hair shimmer in a stray shaft of light coming between the buildings. The women all wore *dupattas*, and very few men grew their hair long here. This could only be the one she sought.

She double-backed, keeping low so if he chanced to look back he'd not notice her. But of the street-vendors, she couldn't hide from. They called out to her constantly, shouting for her attention.

"Goree! Goree!"

There were no other foreign women here, and the long-haired man had heard the calls. He stared straight at her, and bolted around the corner.

Cursing, Jasmine followed as fast as she could, tripping on stones and potholes, snarling at people to move out of her way. She rounded the corner just in time to see the old man outside Cooco's Den react in alarm to someone inside the door of the cafe.

Jasmine didn't waste time asking if it were her quarry; she charged through the door and into the shop, her eyes darting around and seeing a door to the right, where the patrons were all looking.

Through it and up a narrow flight of wooden stairs she went, trying for two at a time when she had the strength for it. She was becoming fatigued, but she couldn't stop now. The man was evading her, and if she lost him now she might never find him again. This might be her last opportunity to track down where Raza had been taken. She felt her fury, allowed it to fuel her ascent.

After several turns and many steps, she burst from the gloom through a doorway into harsh sunlight. It was the rooftop, with a spectacular view of the surrounding area, and the domes and spires of the Badshahi Mosque. But she had eyes for only one thing: the homeless man with long hair stood by the edge of the roof, panting hard. His torso inflated with each breath, deflating until his ribs poked through like a skeleton.

"Who are you?" Jasmine demanded.

"Iqbal..." the man stammered, incongruously.

Jasmine didn't care for his name. She stormed up to the man, grabbing a fistful of his hair and slamming him against the wall of a cupola. His weird eyes were huge and terrified.

"I mean, who do you work for? What do you want with my husband?"

"Not me," Iqbal said meekly, spittle dribbling over his bottom lip.

"Who then?"

Iqbal appeared too frightened to speak, which enraged Jasmine. She literally had the answers in her grasp, and they weren't forthcoming. She struck Iqbal across the face. His head snapped to the side, and she saw a mark on his neck. No, not a mark, but a brand: it had been burned into the man's flesh by a hot iron. Three prongs pointing up from a curved base, a leaf or flame on each tip. It was the same symbol she'd seen on the wrist of the creatures last night.

"What's this, then?" she spat, jabbing her finger against the scar on his neck.

"Jamallan slave," he replied, voice quivering.

Jasmine loosened her grip on his hair. The man was afraid, she realised, but not of her. If he was a slave, then it was someone else – or *something* else – which he feared most. She stood with her back to the doorway leading down to the street, so should he choose to try and escape she would intercept him easily.

"Jamallans are the mafia, yes? You can help me find them?"

Iqbal shook his head, his hair swishing across his shoulders. He stood slightly hunched, as though he were unfamiliar with his own body.

"Who can, if not you?"

Iqbal's strange eyes shifted to the roof's edge.

"Gypsies can," he offered simply. "Down there."

Jasmine tuned into the noise coming from the street below, and amongst the sound of car horns and spruikers she could hear chanting. Stepping to the eave she looked down on the street, and amongst a knot in the crowd was a small clearing in which colourfully adorned men danced.

"Why did they take my husband?"

"They didn't," said Iqbal, chuckling like a child at an inappropriate joke. "Only know where to look."

Jasmine was tired of the interrogation.

"Now, listen here you–"

A strange wind picked up suddenly, whistling across the rooftops and twisting her hair with it. It carried with it a peculiar smell, this wind, so powerful Jasmine couldn't resist sniffing at the air, trying to place the origins of the scent.

"Smell of change," whispered Iqbal, his gold and black eyes observing her intently.

By the edge of the roof behind her, there stood a brass bell hanging by a wooden headstock in an arbor, and beneath it, surrounded by bouquets of flowers, stood a statue of the Virgin Mary. The bell began to chime, a slow and mournful peal. Jasmine had but glanced at the bell for a second, but it was all the time Iqbal had needed.

He shot away, sprinting not toward Jasmine and thus to the stairwell behind her, but to the edge of the roof overlooking the street.

"No! Wait!" called Jasmine, going after him.

But she was too late. Iqbal launched himself from the eave, sailing out into mid-air, arms out like the Christ, head flung back. Despite the whistle of the wind past her ears, she still heard a moan escape the man's lips, as though he were in pain, deep inside.

And of course he was. His body tore itself apart, a violent disintegration into chunks of flesh, pieces flying in all directions. To Jasmine's astonishment, the man's dismemberment wasn't the end of the spectacle, for the pieces of his body flung in every direction sprouted arms and legs, long thin tails shooting out from the amorphous blobs. In mere seconds, Iqbal had fallen apart and in his place, falling across the space above the crowded street, were a troop of monkeys, their faces pushing out from muscle and skin, golden eyes rimmed in black flashing open. Their hands caught the myriad wires looping from one side of the street to the other, swinging themselves in arcs and clutching at their life-lines with fully-formed hands and feet. Others simply sailed the rest of the distance to land heavily upon the rickshaws, bouncing off the vinyl canopies and onto the ground, startling the market patrons before ambling quickly out of sight.

The entire transformation took only a moment, and was over before Jasmine could process what she'd just witnessed. One moment the strange man had been standing before her, the next he'd be undone in a suicide leap, his body mutating into a gaggle of monkeys who escaped amongst the crowd below. Those on the wires had slung themselves along the electrical wires and disappeared through second-storey windows or into trees.

"What the hell is happening here?" said Jasmine to herself.

Not a single person on the street had been watching the skies at the moment of the monkey-man's miracle, reacting only when the critters had landed amongst them. Brass bells chiming in rhythm caught her attention, so she refocused her energies to where Iqbal had suggested she should.

"Gypsies," she muttered, and spun on her heel for the door.

At street level, the roof Iqbal had made his leap from seemed dizzyingly high. Jasmine pushed the scene to the back of her mind and followed the sound of the chanting and bells, pushing through the crowd and ignoring the protests and reprimands for her lack of courtesy.

There were five gypsies, and all bar one had shaved heads, a curled turban on each revealing a bald pate in the centre. But for a single bolt of black cloth wrapped around waists and slung over shoulders, the only item of clothing they wore was a red sash knotted at the hip. But of adornments there were plenty: clusters of brass bells circling their ankles and shimmering as they stamped their feet in dance, charms and amulets on leather thongs about their wrists and necks, rosaries of red pom-pom balls called *ghanas* slung across their shoulders and looping down over their chests. And this was not all: hastily applied makeup completed their look, white chalky foundation with a crimson line of clay streaking down the bridge of their noses from under their turbans.

In their hands they carried musical instruments of long oxen horns, hollowed into aerophones. At her approach, one of the gypsies raised his instrument high into the air and blew into it, disturbing the market atmosphere with his trumpeting. The young men circling the gypsies roared in approval.

"Excuse me," Jasmine said, trying to squeeze through the tightly knit crowd. When the men remained belligerent, she became more frustrated. "Get out of my way!"

The men begrudgingly obliged, staring at her in fascination.

She ignored the gawking, eyes only for the gypsies, and broke through into the clearing. The gypsy before her stopped his dance and turned to face her. Instinctively, the crowd of men at her back collectively gasped, taking a step back. Jasmine stared the gypsy straight in the eye, but when he raised his hand, she flinched. He laughed as he adjusted his turban. Clearly it was important to the gypsies to show their power here, that much was obvious to Jasmine. And it worked; she felt intimidated. By the crush of men at her back, by the formidable gypsies before her, by the spectacle of a man exploding into a gaggle of monkeys in the sky. She was frightened; she felt no shame in admitting that to herself.

"Do you know where my husband is?" she said, trying to keep her voice steady.

From the crowd behind her, she heard a man speak up.

"No, lady. Do not talk with these men. Come away, quick."

From the corner of her eye she could see her advisor, a bespectacled man in a cheap suit. He wasn't dressed for the environs. Perhaps he was passing through on his way to work?

She ignored him, addressing the gypsies again.

"You know where he is, don't you?"

A hand from the crowd reached out, groping at her breast. Jasmine slapped at it, spinning around and screaming in fear and rage to be left alone. The crowd tittered, a sea of faces staring impassively back.

"Listen," she said to the gypsy in conciliatory tones. "I just want my husband back, that's all. We don't need to involve the law or anything here. Just let him go, that's all."

She heard the crowd murmuring behind her, confused by her English, beseeching the bespectacled man to translate for them. It occurred to her perhaps the gypsies didn't understand her at all.

"Lady, please," said the bespectacled man again. "It is not safe for you here."

She glanced back at him. The crowd around him were tugging at his sleeves, pointing at Jasmine.

"Enough!" the man spat, trying in vain to shake his beleaguers off. "Piss off, the lot of you!"

It occurred to Jasmine that the man was the perfect conduit between her and the gypsies.

"Help me," she said to him. "Make them tell me where my husband is."

"It's not safe..."

By now, the performance had ceased altogether, the last of the gypsies rattling a cow-bell before coming to a standstill. All four of them were studying Jasmine intently. Then the one closest broke into a disarming grin.

"We can help, yes," he said cheerfully, in English.

Behind her, she heard the bespectacled man groan.

"You're in it now, lady."

"How much, miss?" someone called from the crowd. "One hour, how much?"

The gypsy scanned the crowd, amused by the growing sense of disarray. His eyes sparkled as they returned to Jasmine.

"She is not a prostitute," the bespectacled man shouted at the crowd as it jostled forward, eager to see the developments now it had decided she was a wanton woman.

For his chivalry, the man was savagely slapped across the back of his head, his glasses dislodging from the blow. He caught them in time but without their vision he was powerless to avoid the fist driving into his nose. Blood arced through the air, splashing onto Jasmine's arm. Within seconds, a full-scale brawl had erupted behind her as the men in the crowd fought one another, fists and feet flying in every direction to inflict damage on one another.

"Come now, quickly," the gypsy said, beckoning her to follow whilst the crowd were distracted.

Through the streets of Shahi Mohalla she was led, the locals staring at her hair. She felt self-conscious about it, but there was nothing to do but abide the attention as she didn't have a covering.

"He's this way? My husband?"

"We don't have him, daughter of Eve," the gypsy confessed. "I am taking you to someone who can help you."

Distraught by the deceit, Jasmine stopped in her tracks.

"What is it with you people?" she nearly shrieked. "Why can't anyone give a straight answer here?"

The gypsy turned to her, his eyes blazing with fury. It gave him the appearance of being taller, more formidable. There was wisdom beyond her grasp illuminating in those dark eyes.

"The Monkey-Man said you could help me," she said timidly, rubbing her arm uneasily.

"And I can," came the reply. "But I have told you: we don't have him. I am taking you to people who can help you better than I. Only I can take you to them. But it requires payment."

Jasmine fished her traveller's wallet from under her shirt, unzipping to show him the rupee notes folded inside.

"Name your price."

The gypsy smiled, almost pityingly.

"Your hair."

Jasmine was confused, thinking perhaps he meant something was tangled in her locks.

"How much?" she persisted.

When the gypsy reached out and ran his calloused fingers through her hair, she finally understood.

"Isn't money good enough?"

"No," the gypsy said, unsheathing a blade from within his red sash.

"Wait, wait, wait," sputtered Jasmine, backing away.

The gypsy shrugged, and began to walk away.

"Okay then!" shouted Jasmine. "But why? Why my hair?"

"For decoration on my horn," he replied, holding his instrument up. "I will be the envy of all gypsies if I have yellow hair decorating it."

As unusual as it seemed, Jasmine could see the sense in it. Since arriving in Pakistan, everyone had been in awe of her blonde tresses. Something she took for granted back home in Australia was envied and prized here.

"Just this much," she said, holding out a considerable hank of hair. "This much only."

"Deal," the gypsy said, reaching the blade up to

her scalp.

She felt the cold metal slide against her skin, followed by the sawing of strands of hair.

"I fucking swear, if this is a joke, you're all dead," she promised through gritted teeth.

The gypsies all laughed, high-fiving one another.

"She has spirit, Dhōkhā," one said, unabashedly impressed.

The deed done, she felt at the spot of the severing. The stumps of her follicles were spiky to the touch, a patch about the size of a thumbnail. It wasn't much in the way of payments, she thought, but Dhōkhā the gypsy was pleased with the prize. He wasted no time tying it to the end of his oxen horn with a piece of leather strapping he stripped from an amulet around his neck. The lock of hair freshly attached, he proudly held the instrument aloft, the golden strands of Jasmine's hair ablaze in the sunlight, and sounded the horn in triumph. It echoed through the streets like a warning.

Around corners and down laneways they continued to lead Jasmine, chatting excitedly amongst themselves at their newly acquired possession. Jasmine idly debated with herself the wisdom of perhaps using the remainder of her head of hair as further currency. It certainly seemed to hold more value than her pouch of rupee, if these gypsies were anything to go by.

The laneway they were currently in had narrowed until the walls either side touched their shoulders when they walked its length, a channel of sewerage dividing the path beneath them so they had to walk with a foot either side of the drain. From the windows above small children poked their faces, giggling at the troupe of gypsies and *goree* gracing their neighbourhood.

Dhōkhā produced a small glass vial, and when he uncorked it, the smell of peppermint oil wafted out. Though strong, it was much preferable to the stench of shit. He tipped the oil into the well of his palm, and having passed it around to his brethren to do likewise, began to smear it over his arms and legs, wiping the last vestiges across his forehead, smearing the clay line down its centre.

Daylight became scarce, so Jasmine took to feeling the walls with her fingers and hoping her footfall didn't find the drain. A shoe full of raw sewerage was the last thing she needed right now. The buildings closed overhead, the only light spilling from behind. The sound of children, and of street life, had also ceased. She could hear the breathing of the gypsies before and behind her. A corner ahead revealed a blush of incandescent light coming from a single bulb hanging from a bracket mounted to the moss-covered brickwork. Beneath it was a small wooden door, a symbol burned into the surface.

"What's this?" she asked.

"The Arms Bearer," one of the gypsies said, and when she looked bemused he pointed at the symbol.

"Not that," she said irritably. "I mean, what's this door for? Where does it go?"

"To answers."

"I'm not going in there," Jasmine said with resolve.

The gypsies all looked at one another. Did they communicate telepathically, Jasmine wondered. Could they read each other's expressions so succinctly, even in this dim light?

"We said we would help," one said, looking at her impatiently.

"This is help," finished Dhōkhā, the gypsy with the lock of her hair tied to his instrument.

"You go first, then," she challenged, feeling the damp and cold prick at her skin. The chill was beginning to give her a headache.

"So be it," Dhōkhā said, not hiding his disappointment.

Jasmine couldn't care less if they'd thought more of her. She'd seen people die, or transform into animals. She wasn't taking any chances here.

The door creaked open, revealing a stairwell descending into pitch black darkness.

"Turn the light on."

"There is no light," the gypsy informed her, laughing lightly. "These people like the dark."

"*These people*," quoted Jasmine incredulously.

"Come," Dhōkhā sighed, hunching down to fit through the doorway.

Jasmine followed suit, noting the other gypsies waited out in the narrow laneway. She could see their legs illuminated by the bulb, and before she'd descended into total darkness, one of them rubbed his hands together for warmth. It pleased her to witness their discomfort, to know despite appearances, she wasn't alone feeling the ill-boding of the place.

Without light to see by, it was inevitable Jasmine would bump into her guide if he stopped on the stairs without warning, which he did. Her face bumped into his bare back, the scent of sweat and dust filling her nostrils before she could jerk her head back.

"What's wrong?" she whispered fretfully.

"Nothing," came his disembodied voice in the darkness. "Can you hear them?"

Jasmine strained to listen, but all she could hear was the blood rushing through her temples. The thin air of the subterranean stairwell made it difficult to breathe. The overpowering perfume of peppermint didn't help, either.

"Hear who?"

"They're in prayer," the gypsy said, yawning. "We should wait."

"I can't hear anything."

"My hearing is... sensitive. I can hear through the walls. When they finish, I will introduce you. They are nice."

Nice wasn't how Jasmine would describe kidnappers, but then she recalled Dhōkhā had never said these were the ones who had Raza, only that they could help. She felt like she was on a merry-go-round, getting nowhere fast.

"Who are they?"

"They are the *Bhaai Chaara Chuhai*," said Dhōkhā. "The Order of the Chuwa."

"Are they like a church group or something?"

He chuckled. "Something like that."

Jasmine mused on the gypsy's words, when it suddenly occurred to her she was familiar with one in particular.

"I know what chuwa are," she said darkly, recalling the knife tucked into the sash tied at her guide's waist. It would take a hell of a guess to claim it when she was blind. Dhōkhā would know her intent long before her fumbling hands could close over the hilt. "Rat-people."

The gypsy fell quiet. She could sense any vestigial trace of humour in the man drain away.

"The daughter of Eve thinks she knows all, eh?"

She didn't like the tone of his voice. It was patronising, underscored with menace. Her body was rigid with fear, her breathing laboured. She tried to calm herself, to regulate her heart-beat. Her eyes had adjusted to the gloom enough to make out the hunched figure of the gypsy in front of her. He crouched stock-still, and if she hadn't known better, she would have sworn he was a statue carved from stone.

"Listen," she said, her voice reedy with fear. "I'll give you my whole head of hair if you help me get Raza back from these people. Okay? His name is Raza. That's all I want. I don't care whatever these people are–"

A rattle of chain in the shadows beyond the gypsy silenced her bargaining.

They weren't alone, that much was apparent. Whether Dhōkhā had been aware of this was irrelevant; something wielding a chain had sat patiently listening the entire time to the two of them, and now it had decided to make its move. After it had been revealed she knew what these creatures beyond the walls were, no less.

"Something's here with us," she whispered.

"The Arms Bearer," Dhōkhā replied, his voice

loud in the terrible silence of the stairwell. "Did you wipe that blood off, from the man with the glasses?"

Jasmine frowned. The fight on the street, Mr Spectacles defending her honour and taking a blow to the face for it. His blood landing on her arm. She ran her fingers along her skin until she felt the droplets.

The gypsy chuckled softly, filling her with a sense of dread.

Jasmine felt for the steps behind, scrambling to scoot up them to the relative safety of the narrow laneway. She'd fight the gypsies to make the main road if she had to, rather than face whatever lurked down here in the darkness.

A hand grasped her ankle, so she kicked at it with her free foot. Dhōkhā was strong, however, dragging her down the stairs with ease. She screamed, pedalling her legs to shake him off, but the man reached down and took her by the arm, his fingers digging into the soft flesh of her armpit. The pain made her convulse, arching her back, affording Dhōkhā a better grasp on her stiffened leg.

Jasmine felt herself hauled from the floor and swung through the air, landing on her back, slightly winded.

From the inkblot shadows in the corner emerged an ominous shape, wheezing and sniffling. As it rushed forward, arms outstretched, Jasmine scuttled away from it. It ceased its advance with the sound of a chain snapping taut. It was a monster, no doubt, an unflattering caricature of the creatures who had taken Raza. Its ragged ears were the size of dinner plates, sticking out the side of its balding head, and where it should have had a snout was a ruin of exposed nostril cavities and receding gums, broken incisors plunging from a diseased maw. Its wild eyes rolled in their weeping sockets, suggesting the creature responded to sound and smell alone.

"Holy shit..." gasped Jasmine, her skin tingling with goose-flesh.

The creature was an unholy parody of the human condition, chained by a thick metal collar down in the basement of a cult of beast-men. It strained at its bonds, eager to fall upon her and, doubtless, devour her. The veins of its throat were thick ropes, coiling up to a skull-like visage. On the side of its neck was the raised flesh of a scar, branded there by hot iron. It was exactly the same mark as on the door at the stop of the stairs.

Only now was she aware of a flickering in the chamber. Dhōkhā had, at some stage during her ordeal, lit a small torch on the wall, the flame guttering fitfully in the thin air. By it Jasmine could easily see the monster reaching for her. It looked diseased, and certainly deranged, clawing at the concrete despite the chain which kept it out of reach of her. The monster wailed and gnashed its teeth, its tongue curling toward her when it let loose a hideous screech. Jasmine's hair stood on end at the sound.

"What the hell is it?"

The gypsy laughed lightly.

"It is magnificent," he said.

The monster raised its head, sniffing the air, its ruined nostrils closing and opening obscenely. Perhaps it could smell the gypsies waiting upstairs, thought Jasmine?

"You knew it was here," said Jasmine. It was a statement, not a question.

She felt a hand press to her back, but too late she realised the significance. Dhōkhā shoved her forward and – in an effort to avoid stumbling into reach of the

monster – Jasmine twisted her ankle, the same she'd injured when the rat-people had taken her husband. She cried out as she went down, the monster's claws raking across her clothes, hideous jaws slavering above her face, spraying drool across her.

Without a word, Dhōkhā departed, casually ascending the stairs. Jasmine screamed for him to return and help her, but they were wasted words. She was alone, and the monster was tearing at her clothing. Soon its claws would be in her flesh, and she'd be pulled apart. There'd be no miracle of the monkeys for her: she was human, a daughter of Eve the gypsy had said. She was, simply put, about to die.

Her shirt torn in half, scratches welling blood across her torso, the monster found its mark, sinking its incisors into her side, its teeth puncturing her skin with sickening ease. Jasmine screamed herself hoarse from the pain, nearly blacking out when she was tossed aside as the creature shook its head to and fro. She felt her flesh tear open as she skidded away from its jaws.

She was behind the thing now, deep in the perimeter of its confines. The pain of her injuries blinded her, bursts of colour appearing in her vision, obscuring the monster. She heard it snuffling around her, lapping at the blood oozing from her side, its rough tongue sliding across the flesh of her waist. The chain made a rhythmic tinkling sound as the monster undulated its head to feed.

She reached her hand out, feeling the cold chain, closing her fingers through the links. With monumental effort she heaved herself into a sitting position, throwing the chain around the monster's neck as she did so. It launched itself away from her belly, hissing horribly, but Jasmine continued to swing the chain, looping it around the creature's neck until the links locked together, refusing to slip loose when the monster struggled against them.

Jasmine rolled sideways out from under the beast, gritting her teeth as she forced herself to kneel beside it. She now had the chain in both hands, yanking hard enough to pull the monster off balance, a strangled cry escaping its bloodied lips.

Jasmine wrapped the chain around her arm,

hooking it under her elbow, tightening the loops around the beast's throat. It thrashed wildly, dragging Jasmine across the floor, slamming her against the wall. She held fast, snarling from pain, the colours before her eyes becoming more intense, more lurid. She was going to pass out soon, she felt it. If she did, she was finished; she'd be eaten alive.

The monster gurgled, face-down on the floor jerking its body to throw Jasmine off. Finally, it fell still, its tongue uncurling from its maw to lay in the dust, those terrible sightless eyes misting dark red.

The chains rattled to the floor. She fell back, groaning, hands slippery as they tried vainly to press closed the wound on her side. She could feel the blood pumping through her fingers.

A crack of light appeared in the wall, followed by a grinding sound of stone-on-stone as the crack widened to reveal a sombrely-lit chamber filled with people. They peered down at Jasmine, and she saw their faces had snouts and whiskers.

Then she blacked out completely.

CHAPTER 11

Jasmine dreamt she stood alone in complete darkness, with something looming behind her, breathing on the back of her neck. Whatever towered behind, it was covered in wet fur; she could feel it brush the backs of her arms when the hot breath came. There was sense of it moving, coiling on itself over and over in constant flux, growing neither smaller nor larger.

And a voice, without gender, simply announcing: "You are the Dark Star..."

A tide of rats advancing from the darkness before her into an insipid pool of light, crawling up her legs and over her body, their tiny claws nicking her flesh, climbing higher to smother her. She tried to scream, but her throat betrayed her, so the only thing that could be heard in the silence was the patter of rat's feet as they fought for supremacy on her body. They rose like a wave, closing over her head, tumbling into her open mouth, claws pulling at her tongue...

Jasmine woke with a start, warring with the tangle of blankets twisted around her body. When she realised it had only been a dream, she fell back down, gasping for breath.

She was in a bed, of sorts. It curved up and over her, an intertwining of bamboo bound with rags and rope. It made her think of a nest, if anything. Like a bird's nest, but on its side, and clearly affixed at some height to a wall, for when she looked out the opening she looked *down* into a room.

It was full of people, this room. They sat chatting while folding clothing, reprimanding the children when the little ones argued over whose toy belonged to whom. There was a sense of community amongst the myriad folk, sharing stories of their daily activities, enquiring after one another's health.

But they were all chuwa, with those same tell-tale faces: snouts, bulging black eyes, long twitching whiskers. Fur instead of smooth skin. Claws instead of nails.

Jasmine felt her stomach lurch at the sight. They behaved as though they were human, not monsters.

Her side itched, and pulling up a tunic of cheesecloth she inexplicably wore, Jasmine found she'd been bandaged. She'd been tended to whilst she unconscious. Scanning the room again, she supposed only one of these rat-people could have performed the surgery she'd surely needed to survive the attack from the monster in the stairwell.

After carefully observing the room for the better part of an hour, hidden beneath the blankets in her nest, she decided she'd eventually need to communicate with these people. There appeared to be no intention to leave on their part, and certainly no way she could leave surreptitiously, unnoticed.

Gingerly, Jasmine lowered herself to the floor, sliding feet first from the nest. There were others like it, attached to the walls, corners of blankets draped from the openings of some.

Some of the children had ceased playing, strolling closer to stand and stare at her.

Jasmine's side itched like crazy, where the wound was probably trying to heal itself. She felt better than she would have otherwise assumed, given the severity of the attack, but when she tried to walk it was with deliberation, calculating her footfalls so as not to jar her wound too much. Escape was off the menu.

"What's your name?" one of the children asked, a little girl judging by her attire.

Jasmine shrank back upon hearing the girl speak; her voice was human, for all intents and purposes, but the child's face was deformed, her forehead flatter than a human's, her eyes expansive, the iris' huge. When the child smiled, her front teeth reached her bottom lip.

"The child means no harm," said one of the adult chuwa, a woman folding laundry.

Jasmine stared from the woman back to the child.

"Your hair is pretty," the girl said enthusiastically.

"Thanks, I think."

"Come away, child," the rat-woman said, beckoning the child to leave Jasmine be.

The child ran to hug the woman from behind, making her smile.

"Are you its mother?" Jasmine asked.

The woman stared at Jasmine, and sniffed.

"Dhama wants to see you, when you've woken," she said sourly. "Now you're awake."

Jasmine glanced around the room. There were probably nearly a dozen rat-people present, yet none had issued any threats.

"Who's Dhama? What do you people want with me?"

A titter coursed through the others, some shaking

their heads and grinning from ear to ear.

"I believe it was *you* who sought *us*, for reasons unknown," the woman said, gently prising the child's hands away from her shoulders so she could stand. "But Dhama is the one to talk to. He's waiting through here."

The rat-woman crossed the room, ignoring the alarm in Jasmine's eyes as she passed her. She pulled a curtain aside to reveal an open-doorway in the wall, beyond which were hallways and rooms, each brightly lit and filled with activity. Jasmine noted the woman only had three fingers

"Straight down, third door to the left," the woman said airily. "Tell him Velli sent you. That's me, by the way, the same who stitched you up."

She glanced meaningfully down to the bandages around Jasmine's waist. She didn't want gratitude, Jasmine understood, but a little respect. Jasmine struggled with submitting to such an entreaty when the pain and itch in her side constantly reminded what these people were capable of. She peered through the doorway, deciding on the wisdom of falling down the rabbit's hole, so to speak.

"It's okay," said Velli, still holding the curtain aside. "We don't bite."

"Bullshit, you don't," replied Jasmine, and taking a deep breath, she stepped past the curtain and into the warren to face her fate.

Dhama stood upon a podium of bricks stacked five high, listening to the debate raging amongst what Jasmine assumed was a kind of council committee. Velli had entered the room carefree, but Jasmine lingered at the entry, out of sight, wary of the discussion at hand since it trained solely on her arrival to their community. The corridors behind her stank of stale urine, however, so the temptation to enjoin with the debating party was compelling.

No two chuwa were alike, Jasmine was beginning to understand. Foremost, there appeared to be differing mutations amongst them: where some were undeniably rat-people, others were subtle in their abnormalities, with only a hint of the beast about them. The wizened one on the podium, Dhama, was probably the more human amongst them. Despite his small snout and large, flanged ears, beneath his long white beard and the tufts of hair sticking up from behind his balding head he was practically human. His skin was devoid of the fine carpet of fur Velli was covered in, and his teeth were relatively small compared to the other chuwa. His eyes, though, were the size of cricket balls, and black as ink, save for a milky cataract over one.

"Tourists don't just wander down here, Dhama," argued a chuwa decorated with an abundance of jewellery embedded with carnelian and lapis lazuli. "It just doesn't happen. There's something not right about this."

"Aru-Min is right, Dhama!" enjoined another. "Why is she here?"

"Of course he's right, Nangal," said Dhama. "I'm not arguing with the point. Just that turning her away would be unwise for precisely the same reason."

The bejewelled Aru-Min wrought his hands together in frustration.

"But it's dangerous keeping her here," he argued. "Traders and tailors don't even have unfettered access to our community, but this woman..."

He shrugged. Dhama sighed heavily.

Velli pushed herself from the wall, sauntering cavalier to the middle of the room.

"And where would you have her go, Aru-Min? Up there? Untutored? Unprotected?" Velli shook her head. "How very unwise."

As the debate began anew, Velli beckoned Jasmine to enter the room. The chuwa fell silent, realising the subject of their deliberations was in fact present. They turned to watch Jasmine cross the floor to where Velli stood.

"You look much healed, stranger," Dhama smiled at her.

"The name's Jasmine," she replied tersely. "Are you the leader here?"

"In as much as we have one, yes," he said. "And as you've heard, it's quite a mystery to us why you would have sought us. You *did* seek us, did you not?"

Jasmine nodded.

"I just want Raza back."

The old chuwa looked to Velli for enlightenment, who simply shrugged.

"Raza?" said Dhama, pursing his lips.

"My husband," said Jasmine flatly. "The one you took."

The rat-people glanced at one another, murmuring and shaking their heads. Jasmine folded her arms belligerently, tilting her head to one side.

"I know you took him," she said, arching her

brows impatiently. "I was there, remember? I was there!"

The old chuwa scratched behind his ear, sighing deeply.

"I'm afraid you're mistaken–"

"I can tell you I'm not," said Jasmine, cutting him off mid-sentence. "I saw you people. You monsters."

Again Dhama went to explain it wasn't they, and again Jasmine interrupted him. She didn't care anymore if they had fangs and claws and monsters hiding in the shadows. Her life already felt forfeit; she'd use what little mileage she had left to pursue her husband's kidnapping.

"We're chuwa, not monsters," said Velli irritably.

"Believe me now?" said Aru-Min to Dhama, and was promptly told to keep quiet.

Maybe it was the heat in the room, maybe it was her body reserving her strength for her wounds, but either way Jasmine felt drained, her energy ebbing. The light in the room became hazy.

"You need to rest," said Velli, moving to take Jasmine by the arm.

"Stay the fuck away from me," snapped Jasmine.

She stumbled away from the rat-woman's reach, standing on the toes of another and getting a yelp in response. If she needed to, she'd do more than tread on their toes; after all, one of their tribe was already dead out in the vestibule at the base of the stairs.

The corridor was considerably darker, and the stink of urine was overpowering. Despite it, she found herself able to distinguish the various scents arising from the stains on the walls. Clearly these creatures were so base they'd taken to spraying their own urine around their home, the dribbles of which had dried on the cracked concrete walls. With her mind running into fever-pitch, she allowed herself to heed her strongest of senses, which was proving to be her nose right now. The scent of urine, though meaningless to her consciously, toyed with her on a deeper level. She followed the corridors, peering into every room, aware she was being followed at a distance by Velli and the other chuwa. Let them watch, she thought; when she found Raza, there'd be hell to pay.

But their lair was inhabited only by more rat-people, each at some task or another: sewing, nursing, washing, playing with the children. Her appearance at their doors startled them.

"RAZA!" she called as she went, repeating his name constantly.

The search proved fruitless, and a sweat had beaded upon her forehead, accompanied with black spots swimming in her vision.

"Out," she gasped, "I need to get out."

Though she could hear Velli trying to convince her she needed to stay, it was Aru-Min who got her attention, his arm pointed along a corridor. She followed his directions, finding herself in a wide room, a kind of congregational hall, on the other side of which was what looked like a door embedded into the concrete.

"That's the exit," she heard Aru-Min sneer at her back.

Jasmine rushed forward, nearly tripping over herself, her eyelids heavy and her breath ragged. Pain blossomed beneath her bandages, a distracting itch spreading across her belly and lower-back.

"How do I open it?" she shouted, her hands

feeling over the surface for a handle or latch.

Velli appeared beside her, pressing on the floor with her foot as though on a lever or pressure pad. Her furry toes poked from a sandal, the talons on their ends clipping the stone floor.

The door slid sideways, though it was less a door than the concrete wall contracting into itself. It was an illusion, surely, thought Jasmine. But she didn't care for the trick, when freedom was all she wanted.

A flush of fresh air rushed past her face. It felt good to suck it down into her lungs, to renew her strength and clear her head. The monster she'd killed in the stairwell was gone, perhaps buried or even eaten. She didn't know what obscene practices these people were capable of.

Her legs felt wobbly as she ascended the stairs, and when she chanced to peer behind she saw the rat-people had chosen to remain below, framed by a rectangle of orange light as they stared up at her.

The gypsies were gone when she reached street level, and forgetting about the open sewer drains she plunged straight into them, the effluent reaching half-way up her calves. She paid no heed, pushing on, running through the sludge until she'd wound through the maze of alleys to reach the main road. At every turn she'd expected to find the gypsies barring her path, but it seemed the price had well and truly been paid, and they'd moved on.

The hustle and bustle of street life was in full swing, the stars in the night sky overhead barely visible against the wash of neon signs and headlights. Strings of bulbs atop wooden carts illuminated a plethora of wares, shadows of people shifting between them, haggling for better prices. It was a make-shift market by the roadside, replete with a thousand smells of spices and hot oil and charred meats.

Her guts heaved, and turning to the side she let loose a burning stream of vomit. It stung her nostrils. Wiping the dregs of it from her mouth, she considered her next move.

People were staring at her, some pointing and laughing. A black sedan edged past like a shark, the half-mast window showing a wealthy man looking back at her in disgust. The rear lights lit up the crowd and buildings in lurid crimson, the sex-workers in the doorways resplendent in their finest *shalwar-kameez*.

The colour and sounds and smells were pounding against Jasmine's senses with an intensity she'd never known. She wondered if the rat-people had drugged her when they'd tended to her injuries. Whatever they'd given her, it felt hallucinogenic.

A rickshaw pulled to a screeching halt in front of her, the stink of burning rubber making her recoil.

She clutched the handle on the side of the vehicle, trying to hold her head up as she scrutinised the driver. Last thing she wanted to do was jump in with one of those rat-people behind the wheel.

A young man with different coloured eyes smiled brightly back, one eye hazel and the other green. She assumed it might be the drugs in her, but it seemed as though his eyes absorbed all the light of the marketplace. She didn't care, so long as he knew how to drive.

She reached under her shirt, but her traveller's purse was gone. Either the monster she'd killed had torn it free, or – and this seemed the more likely scenario – the rat-people had stolen it. Her hand slipped into her back pocket, chancing upon a folded note. It was only a fifty rupee note, not even a dollar in her own currency.

She hung her head, moaning, feeling defeated. Drool strung down from her bottom lip.

"*Aacha*, no problem, miss," the driver chirruped.

When she forced her gaze up, he had his arm stretched out behind, holding open the rear flap for her. She gave him the money and climbed into the back seat, relieved when the flap closed and plunged her into shadow. The lights of the marketplace had become too much for her.

The little engine roared into life, the jerk of the rickshaw's launch lolling her head against the headrest. Shahi Mohalla receded from view, the rickshaw losing itself amongst thousands of others on the roads.

The trip seemed to take forever, but at last Malika's home loomed beside the rickshaw. Jasmine stumbled out, pushing open the metal door to find Malika crouched in the hallway, smearing mango chutney onto the trigger of a rat-trap. Outside the engine splutter of the rickshaw grew softer as it drove away.

Jasmine swayed slightly as she stared at her grandmother-in-law. It wasn't a term she'd felt comfortable employing before, but with Raza still missing her brain drew comfort from where it could. That, however, was about the limit of it for now, as far as Jasmine was concerned. The old woman had made no attempt to prevent her grandson's kidnapping, and here she was however many hours or days since and she was obsessing over the damn vermin again.

"Wrong fucking rats to be worrying about," snarled Jasmine.

She tore up the stairs to the room she and Raza shared, slamming the door shut and flicking the light off. After a moment she could hear Malika shuffling outside on the landing, see her shadow in the crack beneath the door.

"Jasmine-ji? Are you okay, *jannu?*"

Jasmine ignored the old woman, even when she lightly knocked on the door.

There was a prolonged moment of silence, wherein Jasmine had expected the woman to simply open the door and enter. But eventually the shadow beneath the door withdrew.

"I'll make some tea, okay?" came the old woman's voice, ostentatiously making sufficient noise for Jasmine to hear her descent down the stairs. "You can come down if you feel like it, or I can bring it up."

Then Jasmine was left alone with her thoughts, hugging her knees in the darkness and hoping the wound in her side wasn't infected.

CHAPTER 12

A killer toothache woke Jasmine from her slumber. Her entire face felt like it had been pummelled.

The small mirror propped above the washbasin in the bathroom revealed the cause of her pain: her front teeth were much larger, pushing down from her swollen gums. Tapping them with her nail to be sure they were real, she felt the vibration up into her skull.

"What the hell..."

Then she made eye contact with her reflection, gasping aloud.

Her eyes had changed, too, her iris's darkening until they were practically indistinguishable from her pupils. It made her eyes look huge.

She unwound the bandage around her middle, worried at what she might beneath, noting the wraps closest to her skin were stained with blood and fluids. Remarkably, the wound had healed entirely, leaving nought but a shiny pink scar branching across her flesh. She felt fine, too, but for the ache in her mouth.

Staring into the mirror at the changes wrought upon her, she could only shake her head.

"Jasmine, you idiot, what have you done?"

Taking the stairs three at a time, she rushed into the kitchen, rummaging madly through the drawers with one hand while the other held her jaw.

"What are you looking for?"

It was Malika, standing in the doorway. Her presence irritated Jasmine, so she ignored the old woman.

"Did you find him?"

Jasmine stopped, leaning against the counter, her back to Malika.

"No, I didn't find him. I need pain-killers."

Malika opened a top drawer beside the refrigerator and placed a packet of pills on the counter beside Jasmine.

"Thanks," said Jasmine reluctantly, breaking a few from the blister-pack and downing them without water.

She walked to the front door.

"Are you going to the police now, Jasmine?"

She swung the door open.

"I have to talk with someone first."

She pulled the door shut behind her, not before taking final stock of Raza's grandmother and noting the hollow expression she wore. The woman looked like she'd been emptied of all emotion. It made Jasmine feel more alone than ever.

The driver of an auto-rickshaw outside sat up, and instantly she recognised the man with heterochromia, his eyes more vibrant by the light of the day, as though super-charged by the sun. The thought made her smile, of humans who could store ultra-violet like they were batteries, but then she'd seen a man turn into monkeys and a community of rat-people play politics, so why not?

"What are you doing here?" she asked him.

"Waiting for you," he replied.

"Fair enough," she said, squinting as she looked up and down the street. "I do owe you for last night's

trip, I suppose."

She fished out some notes she'd found hidden in her luggage upstairs, and paid the driver.

"This is too much," he said.

"I like your honesty, but it's for the whole day."

Jasmine swung herself into the back of the rickshaw and directed him to return to Shahi Mohalla.

"What's your name?" she called out over the sound of the wind and the engine.

"Imran. It means prosper, *hai'na*."

"You can be my lucky charm, then," Jasmine said grimly, sitting back to enjoy the ride.

The door with the Arms Bearer mark swung open at her touch, the gloomy stairwell taking her down to where she'd been attacked and, desperate to save her own life, had killed the creature. On her ill-fated first visit she'd been unable to see the fissure which delineated a hidden door in the brick wall; now, either without the distraction of the monster or because of her changing eyes, she could clearly see where it stood, the same door she'd exited the rat-people's lair after she'd been healed.

Her hands felt for a crevice, or a handle, and remembering how Velli the rat-woman had stood upon meaningfully on a spot on the floor, Jasmine felt around with her toes for a lever or something, but the floor was flat and featureless.

"It is locked," said a voice in the shadows to her left.

She startled, ready for another fight to the death. Into the light stepped one of the rat-people she'd encountered previously, the one with the excessive necklaces and bracelets of precious stone.

"Geez, you scared me," she said, exhaling from her nose. "Aru-Min, right?'

He nodded, looking her slowly up and down.

"For our safety," he said.

"What is?"

Aru-Min nodded at the wall.

"It's locked for our safety."

Jasmine inspected the wall again. Why on earth would such people need to feel protected? They were the monsters, not she. She'd no sooner had the thought than she recalled the scene with Ahmad the gangster, and how callously he'd shot the beggar-woman. The little boys with stumps for arms at the airport flashed in her mind.

"Yeah, fair enough, maybe," she conceded. "I just want to talk with Dhama."

The chuwa approached steadily with a smug smile, arms crossed behind his back as he walked right up to her. Jasmine stood her ground, hating how he smiled when he simply stopped and rapped lightly on the wall.

"Of course," he said sardonically.

This time Jasmine heard bolts sliding aside before the wall melted into itself. The amber-tinted room beyond was slowly revealed, and although she felt repulsed by the people within, and the underlying stench of urine, she couldn't help but feel a sense of warmth and contentment at the sight of their community.

The little girl who had tried to befriend her when she'd first awoken here perked up at the return of their visitor.

"She's back!"

The girl was having her hair braided by a woman Jasmine didn't recognise, whose snout was longer than any of the other people she'd seen thus far. It filled Jasmine with a sense of terror.

Aru-Min's whiskers itched the back of her neck as he leant in to murmur in her ear.

"Dhama's old, and soft. He holds too much to the idea that covenants can protect us. We've been here a long time now, we're comfortable. Be sure that whatever you decide where you stand, it doesn't threaten that."

When she turned to look at him, he had something like hate in his eyes.

Without a word she stalked across the room and into the corridors, watched carefully by the rat-man.

She found the wizened old chuwa at the very far end of their expansive warren, engaged in trade with a man who looked very much human. When he saw her approaching, the human looked aghast at her, his eyes going from her hair down to her face. He dropped the bolts of cloth from his hands, and Dhama, despite his years, caught it with lightning-fast reflexes.

He followed the human trader's eye-line to Jasmine.

"Do not worry about her," he said to the man.

Velli, who'd had her back to Jasmine's approach, turned on her heel and cocked a brow.

"You shouldn't be back here," she said archly.

Dhama carefully took the remaining cloth from the trader, patting him on the shoulder to snap him out of his shock.

"We'll take them all," he said, smiling.

The man pointed at Jasmine. *"Goree."*

"We know, it's..." Dhama paused. "It's complicated. We'll see you again same time next week?"

The human nodded dumbly, absentmindedly reaching around for his satchel. Velli pressed a wad of money into the man's hands, looking reproachfully at Jasmine. As she escorted the man away, presumably to another entry point unknown to Jasmine, Dhama selected a fold of clothing from the wares they'd purchased from the vendor, and shuffled to where Jasmine stood.

"You think it strange we trade with humans? You think everything we wear, everything we eat, we make ourselves?"

He shook his head slowly, as if talking to an imbecile.

"There is much you do not understand."

"You got that right," Jasmine said petulantly. "Look at my face! What the hell is happening to me?"

He proffered her the fabric in his hands.

"You should try to dress more local, hide your hair."

She slapped the garments away.

"I'm deformed or diseased or something!"

"No, not diseased," Dhama said forlornly. "You have been bitten. You should not have been in its reach, for the Arms Bearer's bite is especially virulent."

"He pushed me, that damned gypsy," growled Jasmine, fighting the urge to punch a wall.

Dhama narrowed his eyes at her.

"Gypsy?"

"Yeah, he brought me here, in exchange for my hair."

Jasmine saw the way the old chuwa was looking at her.

"Why? What is it?"

"Nothing, I suppose," he shrugged. "But there is nothing I can do for you, Jasmine. I cannot reverse your transformation."

His disclosure was the last thing Jasmine wanted to hear. Now she really felt like punching holes through the walls.

"So that's it, is it?" she said venomously. "I'm like you: a rat-person? Go around kidnapping people?"

Dhama looked pained. He bundled the stack of clothing they'd purchased and led Jasmine through the corridors of the warren. Barely a passage had been constructed in a straight line, with each corridor curving and interconnecting with others, creating an unfathomable maze from which rooms and chambers led from. They passed sundry chuwa engaged in familiar domesticity, from laundry to cooking. There was even a group watching television, all seated on a plush rug, the light of the screen reflected brightly in their black eyes. Everywhere Dhama led her there was a sense of homeliness. It made Jasmine think of a hippy commune.

"There is another group of chuwa, here in Lahore," he said. "They have ambitions beyond what is acceptable. We live a co-existence with humans, Jasmine, and it is beneficial for all concerned."

"And who are this other group?"

"They are the Jamallans, as we are the Mohallans. They're bitter, always have been. Centuries ago they attacked the humans, and we were split apart. So we watch them, try to stop their influence if we can, but they do grow stronger, Jasmine."

Jasmine reached out and stopped him.

"And they have Raza?"

Dhama nodded. "I believe they do."

"Then I must go and free him," she said, her breath quickening.

"They are very powerful, my girl," counselled Dhama.

"Then you can help me," she parried, almost accusatorily. "You said so yourself, that you lot try and stop them."

Dhama sighed.

"We did, long ago. With a covenant. All in the supernatural realm recognise it. No chuwa can touch a human without consent. But any who bear our mark, well... If your husband bore their mark, then he is rightfully theirs."

"He was scratched, as a baby," Jasmine said, raising her voice. "As far as he's concerned all these years, it was by a fucking fan!"

She kicked at a pile of pots, glad they sounded like an explosion when they tumbled across the floor. Faces peered around corners to see what the commotion was. Dhama smiled reassuringly at them.

"Where do they live, these Jamallans?" she asked quietly.

"I do not know," Dhama said with a hard edge to his voice.

"You're lying," said Jasmine, her voice tremulous with emotion.

"Have you even heard what I have told you?" said the old chuwa, annoyed. "These are not trifling matters you now involve yourself with. At some time in his life your husband has had dealings with the Jamallans, yes? That's why he bears their mark?"

Jasmine gave the question some thought, wondering if Raza, on one of the few trips he'd made to Pakistan in recent years, might have made a pact with the devil. But it made no sense. He was practically a stranger himself to this culture, having been raised his entire life in Australia. His parents had taken him over when he was still a baby.

Dhama saw Jasmine's eyes light up with realisation.

"What is it?" he asked.

"His parents," she said flatly. "His parents must have had dealings with these Jamallans."

"Then he is already lost to you."

Jasmine despaired at the old chuwa's tone of defeat. There was something implicitly calculated about it. At the far end of the corridor stood Aru-Min, smugly watching their exchange.

"Your humanity is precious; you must try to retain it as much as you can now," Dhama advised. "I can teach you how to do this, if you stay here with us."

Jasmine grit her teeth. This was beginning to sound like kidnapping by another name.

"Am I your prisoner?"

"Not at all," the chuwa was quick to simplify. "We have no claim on you, nor do the Jamallans. We are bound by the covenant. But humans are another matter; they have their own laws."

"They're not worth much, either," sniffed Jasmine, thinking how the police had mocked her. "But what about Raza? What will happen to him?"

Dhama looked along the corridor at Aru-Min, who shook his head and ducked through an archway from whence the aroma of spices and sizzling meat wafted. Jasmine's stomach growled from hunger, but she ignored it.

"The Jamallans rarely keep adults alive for long," said Dhama.

"Prefer babies, do they?"

It was a rhetorical response, one Jasmine hadn't intended to be dripping with as much malice as it did.

"All I know is that it's rare for someone your age to bear their mark."

Rare, but not impossible if the Monkey-Man was anything to go by, thought Jasmine.

"Which way is out?" she demanded, peering through various arches, barely acknowledging the activities underway, or of the rat-people performing them. "I'm tired of this crap. I'm off to find my husband."

Dhama motioned her toward one of many corridors snaking through the warren.

"Jasmine, if you must leave, at least avoid the gypsies. Do not trust them."

She laughed derisively.

"Thanks for the belated warning," she said, and was swallowed by the darkness of the corridor.

CHAPTER 13

Imran the rickshaw-wallah was waiting for her when she emerged from the alleyway and onto Shahi Mohalla Street. He throttled the vehicle into the congested traffic. It comforted Jasmine to be surrounded by all the noise and fumes of human activity. When she'd first arrived in the city, the chaos had been overwhelming, but without Raza beside her, and Malika proving to be no support, the hubbub of daily life here was the next best thing to meaningful contact with something other than the monstrous.

The rickshaw crawled through Hira Mandi, past the Taxila Gate to the Walled City, and onto the National Highway, where they were walled either side not by bricks but by trucks. Jasmine loved them, for they were brightly decorated with folk-art, colourful whorls of flowers and birds and even of lovers on the mud-flaps. The air-horns were like the sounds of a circus, blasting for no apparent reason. The wind whipped her hair around, and for the first time she considered actually buying a shawl if not for anything than for practical purposes. She asked Imran where she could get one, and he waggled his head and told her he knew a place.

When he finally steered the rickshaw away from the velocity of the highway, she recognised the neighbourhood. It was where Raza had taken her on their sightseeing, before they'd made their fateful trip through the Walled City to where the gangster had killed the beggar-woman in cold blood.

Imran pushed on, following the flow of traffic down Baans Bazaar, until after ten minutes they'd arrived at a nondescript crossroads, where he killed the engine. She was about to protest that there was nothing of interest here, seeing only a tobacconist, a petrol station, and a car showroom, when she realised there was a steady flow of pedestrians to and from the entrance of an alleyway.

'What is this place, Imran?"

"This is famous Anarkali Bazaar," he smiled, waving his hand as though he were a tour guide. "Scarf and makeup and many things for woman, *hai'na*."

"*Aacha,*" she replied flatly. "Come with me."

The driver seemed more than happy to accompany her, prattling endlessly as they crossed the road and joined the trail of shoppers. Ahead, the alleyway was more street if anything, stretching as far as her eye could see. And all down its length were a variety of market stalls.

There were stalls laden with thousands upon thousands of glass bangles, in every colour of the rainbow. Carts heaped with watermelons, where vendors hacked them in half with machetes, the spilled seeds and the buzzing flies impossible to tell apart but for the movement of one and not the other. There were flat-breads fresh from ovens and kebab meat sizzling in large pans of oil, fresh vegetables weighed on scales and goldsmiths hammering wedding rings into shape.

Imran watched her from his periphery, a proud grin plastered on his face. She refused to indulge him whatever satisfaction he hoped to glean from her. She was here to get what she needed to blend in on the streets, and that was that.

But Anarkali Bazaar's wonders were distracting. She was teased playfully by a group of cross-dressing lady-boys, amused by parrots telling fortunes with the pick of a card from their deck, geriatric men giving head-massages using only their nimble feet.

Slowly, stranger details emerged: doorways whose frames glowed with a preternatural light. Trays of fresh seafood, the wares unlike anything she'd ever seen or heard of, such as a stack of fish with the scales of a crocodile and a multitude of eyes per specimen.

On a windowsill overlooking market crowds were a flock of children, perched on the ledge and preening feathers which had sprouted from the backs of their arms. Across their bellies and shoulders was a fine down, ruffling in a light breeze.

Jasmine frowned, glancing around at the shoppers but noting they were all oblivious to the oddities in their midst.

"Your new eyes, *hai'na?*"

Imran was watching her still, but now she understood the grin.

"You can see them, too, Imran? The children, the doors?"

Instead of confirming, he nodded toward a tea-stand and said: "You see the chai-wallah, *na?* You see him with truth seeing?"

The chai-wallah stood beside an ordinary cart with an urn and a stack of mugs, wearing a thick cashmere *shalwar-kameez* and a *pakol* cap. She'd assumed him

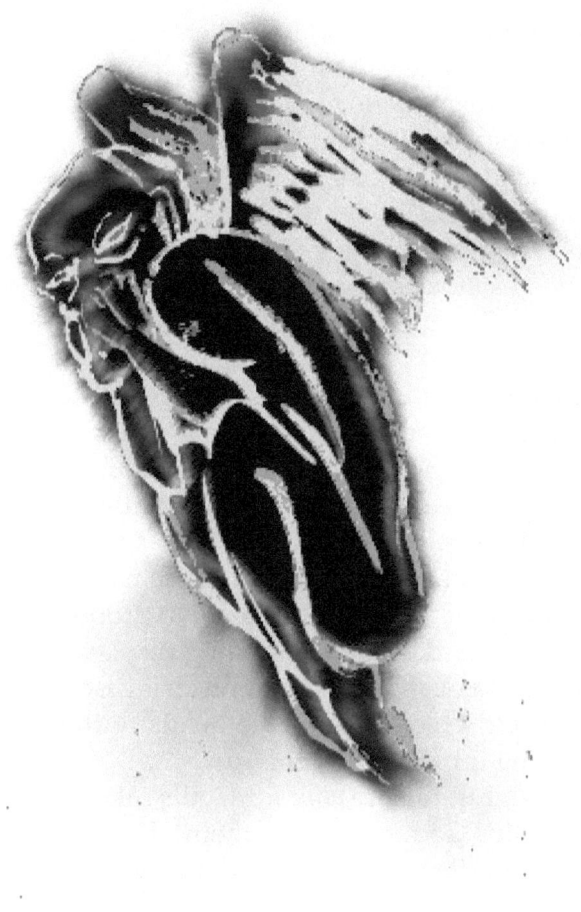

human, and hadn't paid him much heed, but now Imran had pointed him out Jasmine saw the man's skin was glossed with smooth scales. His wide eyes were heavy-lidded beneath the brim of his *pakol,* and a thick indigo tongue like a swollen sea-slug glided over its lipless mouth. As it poured a cup of steaming tea for an unsuspecting customer, the lizard-man made eye-contact with Jasmine and nodded.

She quickly averted her eyes.

"What the hell..."

"It is nothing, lizard serving tea," chuckled Imran. "One time I saw a crow-man giving Azan! Yes! I saw him, up there on a minaret, calling the peoples to the prayer."

Jasmine watched as a man casually walked into a shoe store, apparently unperturbed by the glowing doorway beside the one he'd entered through.

"Can he not see that?" she asked, pointing.

Imran shrugged. "Most of the peoples in the whole world are not seeing these things, these magic things. Not just here. It is the way they are. No problem."

Above the market space a sizzling display of green lights danced crazily, spinning and rising only to fall with dizzying speed toward the heads of the crowd before arcing into the air again.

"Those lights, they're *alive* for God's sake!"

"Maybe for God, maybe for themself," Imran said nonchalantly. "Who knows? But the world is rich with magic and the supernatural, Mrs Jasmine. Always been, always will be. Even here, in my Lahore. Why not?"

They'd stopped at a clothing stall where Imran selected a bright yellow *shalwar-kameez* and matching *dupatta* for Jasmine. She tried to pay for it with the dwindling money she had, but Imran wouldn't hear of it, insisting it was his gift to her.

"For seeing my city with real eyes, *hai'na?*"

She thanked him, and considered all he'd told her.

"And you, Imran? Are you also magic?"

He laughed loudly, startling a family beside them who looked at him like he was crazy. Their reaction didn't bother him in the least. The driver was one of the most carefree people she'd met on her trip to Pakistan thus far, and she felt herself warming to him.

"Magic I'm not having, Mrs Jasmine. Only the eyes for looking the magic. *Aacha?*"

As they left the market, Imran skipped over to a scuffed wooden cart with a trident speared into its top, the tips of which each had an ear of corn wedged onto.

He ordered in Urdu, and told Jasmine this was a sita-wallah. She watched as the vendor flipped back a tin lid on his cart, exposing a dirty pit of warm sand, heated from beneath by a small fire under the cart. He dug into the sand with a long pair of tongs, pulling out two sheathed ears of corn. Once de-husked, the corn was rubbed down with a masala mix and drizzled with a squeeze of fresh lime.

Jasmine devoured the corn, grateful to have something in her stomach at last.

"I've got a question," she said, picking the more stubborn kernels from between her teeth. "The chuwa that attacked me in the stairwell. How could it do that, when I wasn't... well... supernatural or anything?"

"Well, not all the things are hidden, *hai'na?* Some things every person can see. This chuwa, they is one of the things. Everybody's is seeing the rat peoples."

"Do you know the Jamallan chuwa?" Jasmine ventured. "Do you know where they live, Imran?"

He shrugged.

"No one knows. Is secret, *hai'na?*"

And why wouldn't it be, she supposed. They seemed to be the lawless of the two tribes, so they'd hardly announce their address to all and sundry.

The sun was low now, setting behind the buildings. It lent the last of the day a hazy, relaxed atmosphere. Imran tossed his decimated corn cob into a pile of burning trash roadside. The smoke billowing from it wafted languorously across the road, obscuring the oncoming traffic, but Jasmine had no trouble making out the features of the drivers beyond the veil. Her eyesight had developed beyond anything she'd ever experienced in her life. But if everyday people could see the chuwa, as per Imran's assertion, then it stood to reason the changes wrought upon her were also noticeable. She'd had need of the newly-purchased *dupatta* for sure, then.

They climbed back into the rickshaw.

"You like the music, Mrs Jasmine?" asked Imran, twisting in his seat and looking eagerly at her with bright eyes. "Good music?"

Without waiting for a reply, he slipped a tape into a stereo-deck wedged between his steering column and the bubble windshield. A tinny voice blasted from the little speaker, wailing higher in pitch in competition with the violin crescendo.

"Yes, it's wonderful," said Jasmine sarcastically, plugging her ears with her fingers. When she felt a small prick in her ear she yanked her hands free, inspecting the nails, and saw they'd begun to change into claws.

"He is Sonu Nigam," said Imran, unaware of his passenger's self-discovery. "You have him in your country, *hai'na*? In your Ostrilia?"

"No, not really," Jasmine said distractedly. "We have Farnsy and Barnsy."

The rickshaw swerved as it narrowly missed a head-on collision with a bus. Jasmine had become so used to these near-fatalities she wasn't in the least bit fazed.

"Farnsy and Barnsy?" cooed Imran, smiling at her in his rear-view mirror with a little waggle of his head. "Sounds like a good band. Number one!"

Jasmine laughed, despite herself, feeling the infectious and naive joy of the driver. It was so persuasive she decided to simply let herself roll with it, without losing sight of the anxiety driving her to track down her missing husband.

CHAPTER 14

The mausoleum consisted of a marble sarcophagus surrounded by a two-foot wide area for devotees to gather around. Inside the sarcophagus were the mortal remains of a Sufi, a revered mystic long since passed away. That he must have been important once upon a time was evident by the perforated brick walls housing the sarcophagus; walls that, though now bare, were once decorated with tile and precious stone. Those ornamentations had long since been prized free, stolen by those with no interest in the Sufi and his significance, but with a vested interest in eradicating poverty from their lives. Now, the tomb remained largely forgotten but for a few faithful adherents, the dust and leaves piling in the corners of the mausoleum.

The traffic and clamour of street life were but a few feet from the mausoleum, spied through the holes in the perforated walls. The glare of vehicular headlights shone through the gaps, streaking across the tomb in hellish clarity, though no-one passing by bothered to look inside.

"You're early," said a shadow in the entryway.

Dhama, sitting on the edge of the marble casket with his back to the street scene, sat as still as a stone statue.

"So are you, Kha'i," he said.

The shadows shifted, and Kha'i stepped forward into the intermittent light. His hands rested at his chest knuckle-to-knuckle, fingers pointed down, inverted as though in unholy prayer. His jet-black beard was sculpted into a ducktail, and though receding, he still had a full-length of hair at the back of his skull, which he'd meticulously fashioned into a chonmage style. Everything about the chuwa was manicured, and his emerald tunic (for he refused to partake in modern fashion codes like Dhama, who always wore a raggedy *shalwar-kameez*) was of the finest silk.

The rat-man sniffed the air.

"You have the place booby-trapped, then? Your people armed and crouching inside that tomb you're on?"

"No tricks," Dhama said, shaking his head softly.

"Figures," sneered Kha'i, his teeth perfectly filed into points. "I would have."

Dhama slid off the sarcophagus, his feet bare on the dusty floor, and faced his Machiavellian foe.

"I didn't ask to meet with you to ambush you, Kha'i."

"Then what is it you do want?" Kha'i asked coyly, stroking his beard.

A bus sped past outside, its air-horn going off like a carnival ride.

"I want to know what on earth you're up to," said Dhama after he'd waited for the air-horn to fade. "What do you want with the young couple from Australia?"

The Jamallan feigned ignorance with a slight shrug of one shoulder and downturn of the mouth.

"The human was marked, as part of an earlier pact with us, so we have merely claimed what was owed. You should know that, Dhama. It's recognised in our covenant."

Dhama shook his head. The Jamallan had not changed in all the time he'd known him.

"There's no dispute in that," Dhama said irritably. "But you have taken it a step further – you have baited this girl."

"What are you on about, Dhama?" frowned Kha'i. "Have you a high fever?"

Voices outside were close, carrying through to the chuwa. Dhama instinctively ducked down behind the sarcophagus, looking aghast at Kha'i when the Jamallan remained in full view, the lights of the traffic penetrating through and illuminating him.

"I remind you that the covenant between the chuwa tribes cannot be broken," hissed Dhama, peering over the casket to ensure his foe had not been witnessed by the people outside. The humans had moved on, laughing at a shared joke. "It must be maintained at all cost. We have done so for a century now."

Kha'i looked at Dhama with contempt.

"Get up, you fool."

Dhama rose to his full height, wincing as his knees creaked.

"Let us repair the rift, Kha'i, take it back to one tribe... the tribe of our forefathers."

The Jamallan laughed.

"Our forefathers, Dhama? You sentimental dolt. Our forefathers split us into two tribes. And for precisely those same reasons, I will not relent. You would have us all living underground like rats, hidden from the human world. I have a much grander vision."

"And what is it? You would take over Lahore? Recreate the old order above?"

"Why not?" said Kha'i loftily. "With the Dark Star, it is possible."

The old chuwa wrought his hands together, furrowing his brow. What was this talk of stars? He sensed something amiss.

"Usurping humans and enslaving them is not grand, Kha'i. Stop fooling yourself. It is possible to co-exist with the humans. We Mohallans do. We are not hidden. We trade with them, protect them where necessary. It is possible, Kha'i. Even my own clothing is made by humans."

Kha'i spat on the ground contemptuously. His spittle beaded in the dust, beside a discarded soda can.

"I know, I can smell them all over you," he snarled. "You've become weak, old man. Your tribe were once a warrior tribe, one to contend with. You have diluted it down to nothing more than subterranean peasants who would simply wither away without these humans. I call it pathetic."

Kha'i walked back to the shadows he'd first emerged from, snatching a cloak from the floor and shaking the dust from it. He glanced back at his old enemy, hating how defeated Dhama always appeared. It filled him with scorn for the elderly chuwa.

"Be ready, Dhama, there's a storm coming, and when it has passed," and here Kha'i waved his hand through the air as if performing a magic trick, "you will be no more."

He swung the cloak over his shoulders, pulling the hood up over his head. Kha'i ears were especially long for a chuwa, and they poked up inside the hood, creating an unusual silhouette. Dhama supposed the Jamallan didn't care.

Kha'i disappeared into the shadows, leaving Dhama alone inside the mausoleum.

The old chuwa casually shifted the empty soda can with his toes, wondering if indeed humans did have a rightful place upon the earth. A car horn blared outside, startling Dhama. He grumbled as he donned his own cloak and made to leave for home.

CHAPTER 15

Jasmine sat in the dark, staring forlornly at the suitcases on the floor before her, where she and Raza had been packing to return home immediately. Her own, with her clothes spilling out in all directions, and Raza's with every item neatly folded. He was always the organised one between them both. He would know where to start in this impossible quest. She didn't know enough about what was going on to decide where to start. The old rat-man, Dhama, hadn't been forthcoming about the location of the Jamallans when she'd asked, and Imran was as in the dark about it as she.

A scratching at her window sill caught her attention. She didn't care about rats anymore, not with real monsters wandering the streets of Lahore, free to do as they please. Let the rodents have command of the house for a little while.

A gentle breeze teased the curtains, and with it came a familiar scent. It was the same one that had wafted across the rooftops when she'd accosted the Monkey-Man atop Cooco's Den.

She half-expected for a monkey or two to suddenly clamber in through the open window, but instead spidery fingers as white as snow clawed at the ledge, their sharp midnight nails chipping the brickwork.

Jasmine held her breath, a sense of dread washing through her. Malika was downstairs, and the door was closed. Whatever this visitation was – be it a threat or otherwise – Jasmine would keep the old woman out of it.

Spiky white hair preceded the face that rose into view. Like the chuwa, this being had eyes of pure ebony, though it was more human in visage than the rat-people were. It stared at her with cold intensity, before hauling itself through the window in a single fluid and sinewy movement. It was naked, completely devoid of colour, its flesh entirely white like polished marble. From its shoulder-blades there protruded two malformed stumps, as though it had once had wings and they'd been shorn off. They were not unlike the twisted stumps of the beggar-boys at the airport.

Human it might have looked, but Jasmine's gut told her this thing was as far removed from humanity as a dog might be. When it scrutinised her with those lifeless eyes, her skin puckered with gooseflesh.

With preternatural speed it moved across the room, standing across the bed from her.

"Whoa!" cried Jasmine. "You move fast."

She crouched, ready to spring into action should it try to attack.

Another scratching at the window told her the creature was not alone. She chanced a glance in the new arrival's direction, and saw it was an identical being, albeit one slightly shorter and dumpier. Where the first had spiked hair, this one had limp strands hanging to one side of its swollen head.

"The hybrid," it hissed.

"The rat-woman," the other corrected.

The second being pulled itself through the opening and – to Jasmine's incredulity – crawled up the wall as a fly or spider might, completely in defiance of gravity. It moved gracefully, teetering on the tips of its fingers and toes.

"What the hell are you?" demanded Jasmine, her muscles taut.

"Not hell," said the first.

"Never that," the second followed.

When they spoke – though in fact they only ever hissed their words, punctuated with clicks of the tongue – she saw their teeth were sharp and pointed in a bed of charcoal-coloured gums.

They crept closer, slowly edging her into the corner of the room. As they advanced, Jasmine had the sensation that the room shrank with them.

"I am Nakir, the Repudiator," said the first, the taller of the pair. "And that is Munkar, the Unknown."

"We're angels," said Munkar, now hanging from the ceiling with ease. "We question the dead, and take the soul."

"But I'm not dead," stated Jasmine matter-of-factly.

"You're not human, either," insisted Munkar, moving lithely around the hanging bulb and casting a long shadow across the ceiling.

"But I'm not dead!" screamed Jasmine, anticipating their next move.

Nakir lunged at her, clearing the bed in a single leap, halting only long enough when Jasmine's foot connected with its jaw for her to counter-leap across the bed and out of Munkar's reach. She threw a lamp across the room at the taller angel, the cord tangling in its arms as it tried to swat the lamp aside.

Jasmine raced for the door but Munkar fell from the ceiling on top of her, knocking her to the floor. It had her pinned down, its hands going for her throat as if to strangle her. Beside her was Raza's suitcase, so she slapped her hand down inside it, her fingers finding his can of deodorant. She aimed it behind her head and pressed the nozzle, hoping her blind aim would hit the mark. The angel hissed angrily as the deodorant sprayed his face.

Jasmine rolled the creature off, and scrambled for the door but Nakir was blocking the way. It launched itself at her so she feinted to one side, twisting from its grasp.

"You are quick, chuwa, especially for one only recently turned," it said, "but I am faster."

She snatched up a wooden chair, feeling power surge through her limbs. The chair would have been too heavy to lift so easily only a few days ago, but now she could wield it one-handed if she wanted to. She swung the chair at Munkar as the angel rushed her, its pointed teeth bared ferociously. The chair shattered against the creature's head, dropping the monster to the floor.

Nakir dropped to all fours, crawling across the floor with a speed that took Jasmine by surprise. As she swung the chair a second time, the angel threw itself at her, knocking her backwards. The chair fell from her grasp as she tipped backwards out the open window. Her fingers clawed at the curtains, finding purchase, but it was too late: her body weight continued to carry her over the ledge, and the curtains ripped from their moorings as Jasmine dropped two storeys to the street outside, knocking herself unconscious.

The angels crawled onto the window ledge and peered down, hissing in satisfaction. They scampered spider-like down the outer wall of the house.

"Your soul belongs to Malikul-Maut now, hybrid," hissed Nakir, leaning over her body.

At the end of the alleyway, watching the scene unfold, were a group of homeless people. Quietly they crept forward for a better look.

Munkar hissed at them, flashing his teeth in warning.

From amongst the throng stood a bear of a man with a vest and hat made from tattered cardboard. Without a word, he rushed forward bearing a club of discarded timber, one end of which he had set alight. Before the angels had realised his intention, the man struck Munkar across the face with the burning end, the embers and sparks exploding off the angel's cheek and lighting up the night.

"Idiot!" hissed Nakir. "Don't you know what we are?"

The big man stood his ground.

"I know," rumbled Kutta, adjusting the flimsy *kakaul* atop his head.

Around him gathered the rest of the homeless people, numbering nearly two dozen. They were afraid, but their leader inspired unity in them, so they stood behind him, ready to fight to the death if need be. They passed around a burning torch, setting alight all manner of resourced timber to be used as a weapon. The flames grew in size and number, lighting up the whole alleyway.

"If you know we're angels," said Munkar, rubbing

at the sooty spot on its ivory cheek, "then drop the fire and let us do our thing, mortal."

"You're not taking the woman," Kutta said flatly.

"She is hardly a woman, you fool," spat Nakir. "There is *maj-jik* in her blood. She is as good as dead. We must take her."

Kutta jabbed the burning timber at Nakir, striking the angel in the ribs. It yelped, falling back away from Jasmine's prone body.

"Don't defy an angel, mortal scum," hissed Munkar, clicking his tongue in frustration. "You will regret it later when it is your time to pass."

Kutta spat on the ground.

"What's an angel ever done for me?" he challenged. "I live like shit. This woman has filled my belly with warm goats' feet stew, and that's more than you'll ever do for me."

He lunged at the angels again, swinging and striking them with flame, his thick arms never tiring from the task. The angels leapt about, darting to either side of the big man, but Kutta kept the flame swinging, and eventually the angels retreated, scurrying up the sides of the buildings either side of the alley and disappearing over their rooftops.

Kutta turned to face his fearsome congregation, proud they'd stood their ground in the face of the supernatural. Without a word, they bent to pick Jasmine up from the ground, carrying her with such care and tenderness that Kutta's heart ached for his people.

"We go underground," he told them. "Those white devils won't come for her there."

Malika carried the glass of warm milk up the stairs, listening quietly at the door to Jasmine's room. She waited for a sign of activity from within, and hearing none, she rapped gently on the door.

"Jasmine-ji, I have brought you some milk. Please have some."

She tried the handle, and seeing it wasn't locked, pushed the door open to find the room in disarray. The bedside lamp smashed on the ground, a can of deodorant lying beside it. Claw marks across the ceiling. A wooden chair upturned by the window, cracked across the seat. The curtains torn down, hanging half out the window.

Gingerly she approached the window to peer out, expecting perhaps to see her granddaughter-in-law lying in a pool of blood in the street. But it was empty, save for a smouldering branch on the ground.

Malika narrowed her eyes in suspicion, and upended the glass of milk out the window, hearing it splash on the asphalt below, before she returned downstairs to her dark and empty home.

CHAPTER 16

The imposing wall of the Lahore Fort, also known as Shahi Qila, rose magnificently behind the gypsies and their campfire. They were on an open tract of scrub land overlooking the traffic of Circular Road, the tendril of smoke from their fire snaking into the night sky. This was their favoured spot when in Lahore, for the wall at their backs was inlaid with tiles of green, blue, yellow, creating magnificent mosaic narratives depicting the life of kings. Amongst the tableau could be found representations of angels. The gypsies liked to smoke hashish while staring at the celestial sons.

Dhōkhā lovingly polished his horn, admiring the lock of the white woman's golden hair every time his hand worked its way to the end of the instrument.

The other gypsies smiled languidly at him, knowing the pride he took in the transaction for the hair. They stirred the tea as the flames licked up the side of the blackened can.

As quiet as death, three chuwa appeared from the darkness, their black eyes glistening wetly by the flickering light of the campfire. They'd emerged from within the ruins of the wall, between a mosaic of battling elephants and another of a prancing camel.

The gypsies dropped their horns, kicking up dust as they sprang to their feet and assumed fighting stances, knives unsheathed and gripped tightly in their white-knuckled fists.

The most prominent of the chuwa strode forward.

"You traitorous rat," hissed Kha'i without irony.

One of his attendants proffered him a brass bowl, which Kha'i dipped his fingers into. When he withdrew them, they dripped in dark ooze. His talons glistened dangerously as he sucked the ooze from his fingers. Having swallowed the stuff, Kha'i's eyes glowed bright green in the pre-dawn darkness.

"What do you want, Jamallan?" said Dhōkhā, still holding his blade at the ready.

"You know what I want," replied Kha'i, his eyes dropping to the gypsy's discarded horn, and the length of yellow hair knotted to it. "The girl; with hair like the sun."

"Your payment was measly," snarled Dhōkhā. "The woman has one foot in your world and one in mine, rat-man. I have seen to that much."

Kha'i looked back at his attendants, who bared their incisors at the gypsies. The threat was understood well enough by the men.

"Yet, I thought you understood the deal well enough?" said Kha'i, his glowing green eyes fixed again on Dhōkhā.

The gypsies shifted nervously. If the chuwa decided to fight, they knew they'd be on the losing end, and probably fairly quickly, too.

"We did," agreed Dhōkhā. "But you didn't say it would be a *gora*, Kha'i. You only said the Monkey-Man would direct a person of interest our way."

"What's the difference?" the chuwa shrugged.

"You know full well. *Gora's* are trouble. Their leaders look when they go missing. You have put us at great risk, Kha'i. We were seen with her."

Again Kha'i glanced down at the hair of the white

woman tied to Dhōkhās instrument.

"Nonsense!" he snapped. "You damned gypsy dogs don't care about foreign governments! You only have greed on your minds, so don't insult me with your pretend innocence."

Dhōkhā inched further behind the campfire. If it came to it, then the flames would be his greatest ally against the rat-people.

"We're human, chuwa. We don't play by your rules because your covenant isn't for us. You want the woman with hair of the sun, meet our demands."

The gypsies at Dhōkhā's flank smiled smugly at the rat-people.

Kha'i clicked his teeth together three times, and the other two chuwa retreated, swallowed by the shadows. The gypsies scanned the darkness, expecting an ambush.

"You will regret this in time, you curs," hissed Kha'i. "I will rule this city one day, and you with it. Fear that day, gypsy."

Kha'i turned on his heel and climbed through the ruined wall, until the gypsies couldn't see he or his glowing green eyes any longer.

Dhōkhā stood his ground for some time when the chuwa had departed, fearful of their return, and only when the sun began to break the horizon did he finally relax, convinced the rat-people wouldn't return. They were fonder of the night, simply for reasons of cover.

He returned to his place by the fire, taking up his oxen horn from the dirt and beginning the polishing process anew, wondering about the wisdom of his plan as he stared sombrely at the lock of golden hair.

CHAPTER 17

Malika straightened the new curtains to the spare room, the one her grandson and his bride had been using. Where either of them were was now a matter of conjecture, but that they'd been taken by forces beyond her control was certain. Malika felt powerless to intervene, and more than a little useless to be hemming new curtains to replace the torn ones, but what else could she do?

She peered out the window, watching as the breaking dawn stirred the street-sleepers to wakefulness, before closing the curtains on the day. But the room was still light, as though the curtains were still torn from their moorings. A radium glow filled the room, and Malika turned to see a ghost emitting the luminosity. It was a man, younger than she, but instantly recognisable.

"Ansoor, is that you?"

The ghost of her husband appeared as he had when he had died that fateful night all those years ago. The rat-people had come for their grandchild, for Wasim and Bilquee's baby, and Ansoor had fought the beasts off valiantly.

The ghost shook his head sadly.

"No, my love, I cannot return," he said in a voice with crystal clarity.

Malika stood stock still, tears welling in her eyes. It was her Ansoor, after all this time, decades on. He stood before her, and she didn't know what to say. The tears spilled over, streaming down her cheeks. She let them fall. He would see how broken her heart has been without him.

"You know this," Ansoor the ghost persisted, affectionately. "You know I passed on."

"I have been hoping..." her voice cracked with emotion. "I was just hoping."

Ansoor came to her and held her in his arms. Though he was incorporeal, she felt the pressure of his arms around her, hugging her tight. She felt her own body melt in response, as though years of tension were sloughed by her late husband's embrace.

"Shush now," he cooed. "What is done will not be undone. I cannot stay long. But other matters may still be corrected."

Malika was sobbing now.

"I miss you so much, Ansoor. Life is unbearable without you."

"I know, my love, my sweet. You have been strong, all these years on your own."

Malika pulled away, holding onto Ansoor's arms still, and looked him over as lovers do when they've been separated for some time.

"Wasim and Bilqees – they made it, Ansoor," she sniffed, drying her tears on her sleeve. "They made it to Australia as planned."

Ansoor's smile at the news lit Malika's heart. There was no burden in her now, only joy.

"He sends me money. I want for nothing. He is a good boy, Ansoor. We should be so proud of him.

And you should see our little grandson, Ansoor! Well, he isn't so little anymore. He is so tall and handsome. He even has been to visit me here in Pakistan! Three times now, Ansoor! Three! He loves it here. He is married now. She is so beautiful, his wife. She–"

"She is in trouble," the ghost said, interrupting Malika's ramble.

Her mood darkened, and the smile on her face vanished.

"Ansoor, why do you say such things? This should be a happy reunion."

She let go of the apparition, turning to face the curtains.

"My love, it is difficult for me to be here," Ansoor confessed. "I have returned only to wake you to this trouble. Our grandchildren are in the gravest danger."

Malika spun, blushing from accusation.

"You think I don't know it, husband? You think I can't see it, smell it? It's those rats... all these years they have left us in peace, and now?"

Malika began to pace.

"Dearest *jannu*," said Ansoor, "put aside your bitterness and focus."

Malika wasn't to be persuaded so easily, however. For decades she had lived in fear of the rat-people's return. She'd lost her husband to them, in her opinion, watching helplessly as he died of a heart attack in her arms, the chuwa leaving their home in ruin and on fire, scurrying from the wreckage to pursue their only son and his child. Superstitions had run high afterwards, and though none spoke of it aloud, family and neighbours knew full-well the

Makhdoom's had struck a deal with the notorious (some said mythical) chuwa. They had avoided Malika Makhdoom as though she herself had been marked by death. It would be another year before she heard word that her son Wasim had made it safely across the world with his wife and child. It was little wonder the woman's mind had snapped.

"Ansoor! The rats!" she screamed, tearing at her hair, spittle flying from her clenched teeth. "Those bastard rats! They took your life! They took everything from me, Ansoor!"

Even in ghostly form, Ansoor's heart broke see his wife in such despair. He took her by the wrists to prevent her injuring herself further. She fell against him, sobbing again.

"Shush, Malika, no more madness," he cooed softly in her ear. "Come, my love, be strong..."

"I cannot anymore," she cried. "This damned curse on our family."

She pulled away, a fierce look on her face.

"It's all my fault. I have done this."

The ghost didn't argue her point.

"And you can make it right again," he simply said, pushing his spectacles up the bridge of his nose.

Malika's eyes were wide with wonder, her voice barely a whisper.

"How, Ansoor? How?"

"Our *poti*, Malika, our new granddaughter-in-law."

"Jasmine? What of her?"

Ansoor wavered, his ghostly form threatening to vanish.

"I have seen how she suffers for our Raza. She is determined. But Malika, she needs your help."

"I don't understand," said Malika.

Ansoor smiled good-naturedly at his wife.

"Yes, you do. Tell her everything. And take her to the Bride."

Malika's brow knitted in consternation.

"The Jilted Bride of Darkness?" she ventured. "But isn't that dangerous?"

"You know it is," he nodded gravely. "The augur will give Jasmine the advice she needs."

Malika chewed on her bottom lip thoughtfully.

"And the payment, Ansoor? Have you forgotten the price the augur demands?"

Ansoor stroked Malika's hair, his fingers curling behind her ear and tickling the soft skin there. It was something he used to do to her when he was alive, and she loved the sensation as much now as she did then. How she longed to freeze this moment in time and live in it forever.

"No, my love, I have not forgotten the price," he said. "But you can be happy soon. We will be together, as we should be."

Malika pondered the proposal. There was a lot at stake, least of all lives. She looked up at Ansoor with clear resolve.

"Yes," Malika said firmly. "I will do it."

Ansoor smiled sadly and vanished without a word, his departure like a vacuum sucking all sense of joy and hope from Malika's heart. The light from his incorporeal form dimmed until the room was gloomy, save for the glare of the morning sun through the new curtains. As she had been for the last twenty years, Malika was once again alone, but now she had a newfound purpose, and she was determined to see it through.

CHAPTER 18

Dreams of planets, of meteors and destruction, of a black rat and a white rat circling a tree branch she sat upon, gnawing at its wood until the branch creaked beneath her weight, ready to send her plummeting to the ground. Jasmine awoke with a start, expecting to find herself in the clutches of the angels with eyes devoid of all light. She spun around in the gloom, baring her teeth in a snarl. A couple sat huddled by a small fire, but apart from those two Jasmine was alone. She relaxed, noticing the domed ceiling above. It was made from ancient mortar, cracked but held steadfast by the expertise of architects past. No windows, but two doorways.

"Where am I?"

One of the people by the fire turned to look at her, and Jasmine realised it was the big homeless man from the alley near Raza's grandmother's house. She'd fed him the goats' feet when she didn't want them. The man smoked a *beedi*, which protruded from his bushy beard. If the cigarette burned down any lower, there was a chance it'd catch the man's facial hair alight, thought Jasmine.

"You are underground," the man said.

"And you are?"

"Kutta," the man said, pressing his palm flat

against his chest. "And my partner, Farrah."

The woman beside him nodded at Jasmine as she stirred a pot boiling on the flames.

"Where are the angels?"

Jasmine checked the room again, as the mere mention of the pair brought a shiver of revulsion to her. The shadows in the corners of the room remained blessedly empty.

"The angels – as you call them – are gone," Kutta informed her. "I drove them away."

Jasmine sat up fully, rubbing at her joints. She ached all over, remembering the fall from the window. There were scratches and cuts all over her arms.

"You don't think they're angels?"

"They believe it, of course," Kutta said. "Many other people similar to you, they believe it also. But I don't. They're just soul-suckers. They eat the souls they steal. They're worse than vermin. Pardon me."

Jasmine ignored the slight.

"They say they take the souls of the dead to the arch-angel Malikul-Maut for final judgement. But they are liars."

Jasmine got to her feet, stretching her legs and back. She'd felt worse after lesser falls, whilst rock-climbing back home. She wore a long *kameez* top over baggy *shalwar* pants. Someone had dressed her to fit in.

"Where are my clothes?"

"Farrah gave you hers," Kutta said. "Yours were ripped from your fight with the angels and covered in blood, so we burned them."

Jasmine's eyes strayed to the flames; if they were in there still, they were nought but ash by now. It looked inviting, however, the fire, and deciding Kutta and his companion were no threat, she joined them to warm her hands.

"You say the souls of the dead," she said. "But I'm not dead. Why would they attack me?"

"You see? That's my point exactly," grinned the big man, pointing at her. "Wouldn't you think an angel would know the undead when it sees one? And you rat-people are certainly not the living dead. The *zinda-lash.*"

She had no idea what he was on about.

"They won't come after me down here, these so-called angels?"

"No, you should be safe here," said Kutta, stroking his beard and looking into the flames pensively. "There are many of us, and we have fire. I've already hurt them once tonight."

The woman – Farrah – wrapped a shawl around the handle of the pot on the fire, lifting it off to pour the boiling liquid into tannin-stained mugs. She passed the cups of tea around, and Jasmine accepted hers reluctantly.

The tea was heavily sugared, and its sweetness hit home. She felt it calming her.

"Where exactly are we?"

The brick walls looked old, and were caked with chipped mortar, suggesting the grotto had once been tiled. Whatever grandeur the place had once boasted, it was clear to Jasmine it was nothing but a dereliction now.

"It was once a place of worship, but is now forgotten," confirmed Kutta, sipping his tea.

A bundle of blankets in one corner shifted on their own, and before Jasmine could alert Kutta to the miracle two little faces appeared within the folds, peering out at her with big wet eyes.

"Children," gasped Jasmine.

"Yes, there are whole families here," said Kutta nonchalantly.

Jasmine narrowed her eyes, and for the first time she realised it wasn't just Kutta and Farrah with her, but a whole tribe of people, families asleep beneath blankets all around her.

"You live like this?"

"Of course," chuckled Kutta. "You don't have homeless people where you come from?"

"Yes, but I never mix with them," she said rather too quickly, and hearing the words aloud made her feel ashamed. "I mean, we don't..."

She couldn't finish the sentence. Either way, she knew what the truth was: that the homeless were invisible to her, and that choice had always been hers alone. Never had she imagined in all her years that she'd seek refuge amongst them.

"It's sad that we never truly know how the other lives," said Kutta quietly, hefting himself up.

Jasmine could only nod, and watch as the big man shuffled quietly over to the children and stroked their hair until they were asleep again. He benevolently saw to the rest of the tribe, ensuring feet were covered by blankets and water was within reach. It was as though he were their shepherd, and they his flock, the way he tended to the people.

When he returned to his spot by the fire, Jasmine thanked him for his care.

"I should be off now," she said.

"But you cannot," he urged. "Those soul-suckers might still be up there."

"It's a chance I'll have to take. I need to find my husband, and I think I know exactly who to talk to about it."

There was a bitter edge to her tone as she thought of Malika's apathy.

"I can see that you cannot be deterred, Jasmine. If you must insist on going back up, let me show you another way."

He led her through one of the doorways and along a passageway, past sundry entrances with corridors stretching away. Unlike the warren of the Mohallan chuwa, these corridors were lifeless, a dry musty odour clinging to them.

"It's none of these, is it?"

Kutta shook his head.

"No. A long time ago, in the age of Kings, there was a secret tunnel built underneath the Great Fort Shahi Qila," he explained. "This tunnel was used by the kings of the time to flee the Fort in the event of an invasion. The tunnel went underground and came up outside the city walls. Since then, Lahore has spread herself over that territory."

"And this tunnel is here somewhere? It still exists?"

She swatted at a cobweb strung across the path.

"Oh yes," grinned Kutta. "We use it sometimes. It is ours now. We are the new kings."

"The meek inheriting the Earth," said Jasmine dryly.

Kutta smiled in recognition of the phrase.

"So said another supernatural being of great magic," he said.

"That's not from a supernatural creature, it's from–"

"The Bible, I know."

Jasmine cocked an eyebrow, surprised.

"I'm very well read, you know," Kutta laughed. "Don't let the dirt and the rags fool you."

"Something I need to keep in mind," said Jasmine, feeling somewhat foolish for her assumptions. "I can't keep judging books by their covers here in Pakistan."

The big man held up a swathe of cob-webbing, gingerly lowering it again after they'd passed under. Jasmine was grateful he remained tight-lipped about her senseless destruction of the cobweb earlier; it hadn't occurred to her the big man might extend his courtesies to something she considered as lowly as a spider.

"Yes, you'd do well to keep that in mind while in Lahore," he said of her idiom about book covers. "Ah, here it is; the tunnel."

They arrived at another entranceway in the myriad corridors. It was unassuming, though sturdy and well built. Jasmine peered into its black depths.

"It is very straight," she said. "It doesn't curve for at least a mile."

"Your improved chuwa vision can see what I already know from experience," said Kutta sagely.

Jasmine smiled apologetically.

"This tunnel will get you far from the watchful eyes of the soul-suckers, those so-called angels," said Kutta. "Farewell, my friend."

Jasmine hesitated, for she'd not considered them friends and thought it strange he might.

"Please thank Farrah for the clothes," was all she could return.

"You are reckless, and cannot see the dangers

coming," he cautioned. "But you are determined, by God. And I hope you give them all Hell before you are done."

He turned and began his return journey back to his tribe. For a moment she watched him go, and then faced the long tunnel ahead of her, considering his words. He was right about one thing: she *was* determined.

She squared her shoulders and plunged into the tunnel, not sure if she was truly ready for what lie ahead but damned if she'd sit on her haunches and do nothing about it.

CHAPTER 19

As if by magic – and here Jasmine wasn't so sure there wasn't any in play – when she'd emerged from the tunnel outside the Lahore Fort, she'd chanced upon Imran the rickshaw-wallah engaged in a fiery debate about love songs with a contingent of other rickshaw drivers. The other drivers had been green with envy when Jasmine had bee-lined straight for him, and though she'd been cashless, Imran had insisted he drive her home free of his charge, claiming it was his duty and honour because she'd been so good to him. Working as a rickshaw-wallah was challenging, he'd explained, when he was competing with nearly a million other drivers.

The midday traffic was nightmarish, bottle-necking in several areas and bringing them to a standstill. The choking diesel fumes of trucks and rickshaws trapped the heat of the high sun, making Jasmine sweat so profusely she could feel it running down her back.

She laid her head against the frame of the vehicle, consoled by the vibrations hammering through her skull.

Without thinking, she'd begun to sing aloud.

"*Aao saamney,*
Aao saamney,

Kholo di usske na rang maaya..."

Imran watched her keenly in his mirror, surprise lighting his face up and barely able to contain his excitement. When she'd falteringly sung a few verses to herself, he clapped his hands together furiously.

"*Shabash*, Mrs Jasmine, *shabash!* Very beautifully well done. Now you are knowing Punjabi for how long?"

His praise wrenched her from her thoughts, and for a moment she was disorientated as to where she was. When she saw Imran twisting in his seat and applauding her, she grinned bashfully.

"I don't know Punjabi," she admitted. "Only that line. Raza used to sing that song to me, and that was my part to join in."

A ripple of anguish crossed Imran's face.

"The lovers' song," he said, grunting appreciably. "First class song, Mrs Jasmine. You want me to sing it for you?"

She certainly didn't.

"No, please don't– "

Imran burst into recital, his voice melodic and carrying over the sound of engines and horns around them. Her ears tuned into his voice with such accuracy, soon all she could hear was Imran's deeply affecting and sonorous singing while he edged the rickshaw through the traffic. By the close of the song, he'd sung with such passion he was weeping. A box of tissues was wedged behind his seat for passengers' convenience, so she tore several free and passed them over.

"My god," she breathed, "that was..."

"Magical?"

His grin was ear-to-ear as he regarded her in the

mirror, and when she caught his eye they both exploded with laughter. She felt good, bonding with someone again, and she smiled to herself as the traffic picked up pace.

"Tell me about your eyes, Imran."

The driver shrugged.

"What can I say, *hai'na?*"

"I mean, they're not actually *your* eyes, are they? I think I've worked that much out."

He fell silent, mulling something over. She feared she may have offended him.

"I'm sorry, I shouldn't have asked," she said.

"No, no problem," he said, deftly weaving the rickshaw between two trucks and shooting out from between them just as they closed the gap. "It is just sad story, *hai'na?*"

"The best stories always are," Jasmine said solemnly, thinking what she'd need to tell her family, and Raza's parents, if she were to be forced to return home without him. She looked down at her hands, where her nails had malformed into claws, and knew there was no going home until she could reverse her condition.

"Years ago, many ago, I was the rickshaw driver," began Imran. "I worked hard to be. I was born as the slum person, *aacha?* But I did work very hard, too much hard, and then I became the rickshaw-wallah. *Hai'na?*"

Jasmine nodded, listening intently.

"But one day it was a fight, very big one," he said. "This one man, he was cheating bastard. He took commissions too much. Nothing was left for us. The drivers were all too much angry. But what can we do?"

"What *did* you do?" she asked, for clearly this was the catalyst for his present abilities.

Imran became noticeably angry by the memory.

"I went and I told that shit sisterfuc–"

He stopped midsentence and fleetingly glanced at Jasmine, bashful for the outburst of profanity.

"Sorry. I told him to pay us the good amount, or there is trouble for him. Well, he was angry, of course. He hit on me, but also I hit on him. After, his men did beat on me too much. They used the mekanik's tools to take my eyes. They just took."

He made a plucking motion in the air with his fingers.

"They blinded you?" said Jasmine, recalling the armless boys at the airport.

"And beat on me," Imran reminded her, as though it was somehow the worst part of the story.

An air-horn blasted right beside them, nearly deafening her. She was tempted to reach through the rickshaw's side flap and slash the trucks tyres with her claws.

"And your new eyes," she persisted, "these that you see the world with now?"

Imran waggled his head.

"They are belong to the supernatural thing, who did the wrong thing one time by them. So they took his eyes also. But now I have them. A good gift, *hai'na*? Seeing?"

Jasmine was confused.

"Who took those eyes from the supernatural being, Imran? The rickshaw people?"

Imran laughed. The rickshaw took a corner so sharply the rear-left wheel left the asphalt. He'd swerved into a side-street which looked familiar to

Jasmine. They were close to Malika's home; she was beginning to recognise the city's landmarks.

"No, it was the supernatural peoples," Imran continued. "They took these eyes from their own one."

"But *who* gave you the eyes, Imran? Was it the rat-people?"

Imran waved his hand, gesturing for the conversation to finish.

"No, Mrs Jasmine, not them. I cannot accept the eyes from the chuwa. Anyways, it's no problem. Just leave it now."

Jasmine noted the sense of finality in his voice, and sat back against the cushioning. She was tired, and the way Imran had shut down on her irritated her.

"Fine," she said. "Just get me home."

Imran nodded, gunning the rickshaw down a few more streets, before pulling up outside Malika's house. The sun bore down on the neighbourhood, bleaching everything hot white. Of the angels, the soul-suckers, there was no sign.

Imran killed the engine.

"Are you angry to me?"

Jasmine rolled her eyes, rubbing her face with her hand. Soot smudged her palm, the inevitable result of riding in an open vehicle through Lahori traffic.

"No, Imran, I'm not angry," she said, sighing deeply. "I'm just tired with all this bullshit, you know? I just want to get inside and get Raza's grandmother to talk. That woman knows more than she lets on."

She climbed out of the vehicle.

"*Aacha*, if I can just say one thing, Mrs Jasmine," the rickshaw-wallah said, leaning out the driver's space. "Be careful of the people for trusting. Just be careful, *hai'na?*"

Jasmine smiled mirthlessly.

"Yeah, you're the second person to have said that recently."

She mounted the steps to the front door and, finding it unlocked, pushed it open and disappeared inside.

Imran stared down at his hands on the steering-wheel, numerous conflicting emotions flashing across his face. Unable to bear the onslaught, he began to weep.

Suddenly, the gypsies appeared beside him, leaning on his rickshaw to push their smug faces close to his. His misery amused them.

"What's wrong, rickshaw-wallah?" jeered their leader, Dhōkhā. "Why do you weep? Are they tears of joy?"

He scowled at them, which made them laugh harder.

"What do you want?" he asked sullenly.

"Only to remind you, rickshaw-wallah," they said. "You have sight, so use it. Keep an eye – or two – on her."

Imran's mood darkened even further as he shook his head imperceptibly.

"What?" challenged Dhōkhā.

Imran refused to meet their eye, instead staring determinedly at his whitening knuckles on the steering wheel. His body shook with fear.

"No more," he said resolutely. "No more. She is a good person."

Dhōkhā narrowed his eyes at the rickshaw-wallah as his gypsy troupe cackled behind him. He reached out and put a hand on Imran's shoulder, digging his fingers into the flesh. The rickshaw-wallah winced with pain.

"Our little comedian," hissed Dhōkhā. "She could never love a piece of trash like you. Just do your job. You owe us, remember? Keep the *goree* safe from harm."

"And keep an eye on those damned angels, too," said another of the gypsies, his khol-rimmed eyes ogling Imran with unreserved menace. "They've already made one effort on her. A little longer, rickshaw-wallah, and Kha'i will bow to our demands. Then your job will be done."

Dhōkhā slapped Imran twice on the back of the head, an affectionate but domineering gesture.

"You fail us, rickshaw-wallah," he cautioned, "and we take back what we gave."

The gypsy reached for Imran's face, and the rickshaw-wallah instinctively covered his eyes, which brought a fresh howl of mockery from the other gypsies.

They sauntered away, the bells on their ankles shaking as they stamped their feet.

Imran groaned, resting his head on his folded arms across the steering wheel.

CHAPTER 20

Malika was in the kitchen, a large spring-loaded rat-trap in one hand and a butter-knife in the other. She was smearing mango chutney straight from the jar onto the rusted trigger of the trap, double-dipping into the jar to ensure a heap of the gooey reserve was there to bait the rodents. Jasmine made a mental note not to eat from the jar of chutney anymore.

"Okay, old woman, spill it," she demanded, leaning against the counter-top beside Malika.

Malika looked puzzled, and seeing how fiercely annoyed Jasmine was, decided to play along. She upended the jar, the contents sluicing out and landing on the floor with a splat.

"Don't be cute with me!" barked Jasmine, slapping the jar out of the old woman's hand. It shattered against the wall.

"How dare you!" cried Malika.

Snarling, Jasmine pushed her nose up to her grandmother-in-law's face.

"Look at me, Malika! Really look at me! I'm not normal!"

For the first time since Raza's disappearance the old woman took stock of Jasmine, and saw the changes that had been wrought upon her. The young woman's iris' had burst, their colour bleeding across the whites of her eyes and darkening as it went, lending her left eye the appearance of being animalistic.

"Chuwa..." said Malika, the word escaping her like she'd had the wind knocked from her.

The old woman fell back against the wall, her hand on her heart, gasping for breath. She shook her head in denial.

"Now, cut the crap," said Jasmine.

"Ansoor, he warned me..."

"Who's Ansoor?" demanded Jasmine.

Malika retrieved a photo-frame from the wall in the lounge, containing a black and white photo of a family, and showed it to Jasmine. Clearly, the middle-aged woman in the photo was Malika. She pointed at the man standing beside her.

"He was my husband."

There was young couple in the image, and Jasmine had no trouble identifying them as Raza's parents, though they were about her age. In their arms they held a baby.

"Raza."

"Yes," nodded Malika. "His mother, Bilqees, she was barren. For a new bride, in our culture, this was devastating. But I took pity on her, because I loved her as if she were my own daughter."

The house was deathly quiet, motes of dust drifting lazily in the beams of sunlight streaming down from the high windows. It felt as though time had stopped. The old woman held her breath, staring into space. It seemed to Jasmine as though the old woman expected someone to materialise before her.

"Raza said his grandfather died in a house fire, when he was a baby," said Jasmine softly, breaking

Malika's reverie.

The old woman smiled uncertainly. She walked through to the lounge, studying the photos on the walls in gilded frames.

"He was burned alive," said Malika sadly. "I barely escaped."

Jasmine covered her mouth as she gasped. Raza had never divulged such details, if indeed he'd even known. And his parents, of course, had kept it to themselves.

"His heart gave out, and I couldn't move him out to the street," Malika continued.

"Was it in this house?" asked Jasmine, stepping through the archway into the room.

The old woman nodded.

"The chuwa," ventured Jasmine, and again Malika nodded. "But why?"

"There is a belief the chuwa have been touched by the divine, and such divinity has been imparted to them," explained Malika, caressing the glass over the photo of her family. "As such, we look on them as blessed. Rarely are they refused anything. Anyway, it is said that with their blessing, barren brides are gifted with children."

Jasmine covered her eyes with one hand, fighting the temptation to shake her head in disbelief. Her opinion of the rat-people was about as far removed from divinity as one could get.

"We were desperate," Malika persisted. "Wasim and Bilqees had been married a year, waiting for a visa entry to Australia, and there was no child. In our Pakistan, especially in those days, it is terribly important. Neighbours were gossiping, curious about what sins our family were atoning for."

Amongst the litter of frames on a small table in the corner, Jasmine found one of a small boy smiling broadly for the camera, dressed in a football jersey. She recognised it as Raza, probably about eight years old, standing on a sports field in Australia. How was he born if his mother, Bilqees, was sterile?

"It was affecting Ansoor's business," came Malika's voice, croaky with age and emotion. "People avoided his salon. His barbers left, too, thinking the ill fortune of our family might also contaminate them."

Jasmine turned to face her.

"And what's this got to do with the rat-people?"

Malika wrung her hands together, her throat muscles pulsing as though trying to contain her words.

"As I said, we were desperate, so I took Bilqees to the chuwa, for their blessing. I had to do something. Doctors were useless to us, and even the holy men couldn't lift any evil-eye from us. But the chuwa, those divine people, they did help. They have an elixir – a green liquid – which can cure barrenness."

"Bilqees became pregnant after your visit?"

Her anger was showing; she couldn't help it, after all she'd experienced. The rat-people were sounding more like snake-oil merchants the more she heard of them. Jamallans or Mohallans, they were all the same to her, Dhama and his sympathies be damned.

"Yes," said Malika. "We were all so happy. But there was sadness behind our happiness, also. Everyone who goes to the chuwa must make the same promise: in return for the curse of barrenness to be lifted, the firstborn belongs to them."

Jasmine was astonished.

"Wait," she said, holding her hands up for a moment's grace. "You promised Raza to these chuwa?"

She didn't need an answer, and wasn't furnished with one. She paced the room, processing the details.

"What do they do with these babies?"

Malika shrugged.

"It is believed that they are deformed, somehow, to use as beggars. If they look touched by the divine, they earn more money."

"Yeah, that sounds familiar," scoffed Jasmine, thinking of the little boys at the airport. "Fuck, Malika! What the hell were you thinking?"

The old woman was ashamed, hanging her head.

"I wasn't. We just wanted our luck to change."

"And then you changed your mind so they came for him anyway," said Jasmine, piecing it all together. "And they nearly got him, scarring him in the process."

Jasmine struggled to comprehend that a family of four could have resisted a gang of chuwa with ease. It didn't make sense, not in her experience. Even now, standing in the lounge, she could feel the power surging through her, imbuing her with strength she could never have possessed before. If she wanted to, she could easily fend off two humans on her own.

"So why didn't they take Raza, as a baby? There must be a reason, Malika."

Malika shrugged, but when she saw Jasmine staring coldly at her, she rubbed her arms.

"I was given several warnings to hand him over," she confessed, "but Wasim had been accepted into University in Australia, so we hoped we could stall long enough for him to leave. It was chaos."

Jasmine continued to stare at Malika.

"And my dear Ansoor, my poor husband..."

Tears fell, but Jasmine remained unmoved. There was something the old woman was deliberately omitting.

"Did they know about the trip to Australia, Malika? Is that why they came when they did?"

"No, they didn't..."

There was hesitation, as though there was more to the story. Jasmine stretched her hand, feeling the claws extend. The old woman noticed and became visibly shaken.

"Did they know about the trip?" Jasmine repeated.

Malika slowly nodded.

"But not until they attacked us," she said, sobbing now. "They saw the plane tickets. I never told anyone, but I saw them looking at the tickets."

Jasmine paused, staring open-mouthed at her grandmother-in-law. It was obvious by the old woman's reticence that she also understood the ramifications of the revelation.

"So the chuwa knew baby Raza was being taken overseas, and let it happen?"

Malika swallowed hard, glancing around the room again as if expecting someone to materialise.

"I cannot help you fight these chuwa, Jasmine-ji. I am too old. But I can take you to someone who can help. Ansoor told me what I must do."

"Your husband Ansoor? Twenty years ago he told you what you'd need to do?"

"No, only today," said Malika, smiling forlornly. "Whatever you want, it will be yours."

The old woman was bat-shit crazy, thought Jasmine. Conversing with imaginary people now.

She strolled slowly around the room, studying each photograph in turn. There were the old ones, colourless or long-since faded, but there were also newer ones. Raza's graduation from high-school, Fouzia's fifteenth birthday party at a roller-rink, family outings. There was even one of Malika and Raza alone, arm in arm, taken on the steps of the house. It looked like it had been taken only a few years prior, on one of his trips visiting family here.

"I just want things to be normal again," sighed Jasmine. "I want Raza back. I hate it all. I wish we'd never come here."

The photo of the old woman with Raza was in a cheap plastic frame, the words BEST GRANDSON engraved along the bottom.

"That probably sounds awful," Jasmine said.

Malika smiled softly.

"This country can be difficult, even for the people who live here,' she said. "It is especially hard for you, now."

Jasmine looked back at the old woman, whose eyes were still wet from the crying. Gone from her was all the pretension, the eccentricity and oddity. She was a lonely old woman who had practically lost everything, yearned for it all still, and felt completely powerless to do anything about it.

"That's true," said Jasmine. "So let's go change that. You said you knew someone who can help?"

Malika nodded, taking a deep breath to fortify herself.

Imran brought the rickshaw to a halt on an unassuming road, and killed the engine. There was an ominous walled thoroughfare leading away from them, closed off with a steel gate and padlock. It led into a field of dead grass and dust, the Mughalpura Train Yards just beyond. Further down the road were a set of small shops, boys in mechanics overalls sitting out front and smoking. The trees were the same dusty colour as the road and fields.

"Is this it?" Jasmine said, alighting from the rickshaw.

Imran waggled his head.

"Is looking like it has magic in it, to me," he said. "This is a *bhari-jaga*."

"A *what* now?"

"*Bhari-jaga*," Imran repeated. "A place heavy with spirits. You feel it, *hai'na?*"

Jasmine glanced at the solemn gate. In the trees crows cawed lazily. She was sceptical.

"We'll meet you back out here, Imran."

"*Aacha*, Mrs Jasmine," he grinned. "No problem."

She stopped and stared at him, frowning imperceptibly at his cheery countenance. Kutta's warning about who could be trusted resounded in her head.

"It's down there," said Malika, pointing down the corridor of brick.

Jasmine walked over and snapped the padlock off. It came away easily, and she had to admit having such strength impressed her.

The rickshaw driver continued to waggle his head, smiling jovially. Jasmine felt a sense of foreboding as she followed Malika down the passageway. It was cool between the walls, with leafy braches overhead filtering the sunlight. On any other day it would feel like a pleasant stroll, but with recent events it felt as though the walls might close in any second, trapping her and Malika forever. As they walked, it occurred to Jasmine there were no sound of birds in the trees or field beyond the walled passage, whereas out on the road she'd seen songbirds flitting from branch to branch.

At the end was the tomb, sitting in a field, and about the size of a small house. It was in disrepair, and hundreds of years old by Jasmine's estimation. It sat on a hexagonal platform, which the women climbed, the dome reaching almost two stories above them. They made their way inside through a vaulted opening, only to find the mausoleum featureless and empty.

It might have been a place of glories once, but that time had long since faded from living memory. It didn't look like a place of magic, but it certainly felt like one. The hairs on Jasmine's arms rose in response to the presence of something powerful.

"Now what?" she said, looking around at the empty space.

"We go underground," answered Malika.

"There's no door."

Malika looked apprehensive.

"There is," she insisted. "I can't see it, but you can."

Jasmine inferred her meaning, and glanced around for anything that glowed like the doors she'd seen in Anarkali Bazaar. The brick walls remained as they were, as did the floor and ceiling.

"You must be able to with the bane in your blood," the old woman said, approaching the walls of the mausoleum and rapping her knuckles on them.

"Maybe this is the wrong place?"

"It cannot be," said Malika urgently, her fingers crawling desperately across the cracks in the bricks. "It is such a strong *bhari-jaga*. I'm certain this is the place."

The Mohallans had a wall which opened as though by intent, so perhaps this entrance needed comparable influence? She hung her head in thought, propped against the wall by an outstretched arm.

Malika sighed wearily, walking over to the vaulted arch they'd entered through, and stared out at the sun-drenched fields. The grass swayed in a slight breeze.

"It's peaceful here," she said.

Jasmine glanced back at her grandmother-in-law, thinking to herself how much the old woman looked like a spirit framed with a golden glow of light from outside. She supposed it must have taken a strong heart to survive the horrors she had, and to have lost her family with it. The chuwa had robbed Malika of everything she held dear when they had attacked that fateful night.

She lifted the *kameez* Farrah had given her, noting the scar she'd received from the Arms Bearer at the Mohallan's warren. Then her eyes strayed to the cuts on her arm, bright crimson against her pale flesh.

"Maybe..."

Malika turned.

"What is it?"

"Maybe my blood will open it?" Jasmine lifted her arm and sliced savagely into with the claws of her other hand. "Maybe it's not enough to *have* this blood? Maybe I need to start *using* it."

Rivulets ran down over her forearm, dripping to the floor. She angled it so the blood made its way into her palm, where she let it well. Malika looked on intently. With a full palm, Jasmine aimed her hand for the wall and slapped against it, the blood shooting out from under her fingers. She stepped back, watching the bloody print on the ancient brick drip down, waiting for the door to swing open on creaking hinges.

"Damn it," she said, turning to face Malika when nothing happened. "Now what do we do?"

"Look," gasped the old woman.

Jasmine faced the wall to see it had begun to sink in on itself, her bloody hand print distending as the bricks fell into a chasm beneath where the wall stood. An imprint of a doorway revealed itself in the softening brick, and as the pieces fell away into the dark hole, the remainder of the wall stretched like melted cheese after their fallen companions. With the last of the bricks gone into the chasm, the makeshift doorway hardened into solidity again, the rough edges where the wall had strung like melted cheese hardening into sharp stone.

Beyond there was a stairwell leading down into impenetrable darkness, heat as though from a fire emanating up from below. Expecting horrors might lie in wait, Jasmine shifted her grandmother-in-law behind her, as if to shield the old woman

"Okay, let's do this," she said. "Follow me; I can see in the dark now."

Malika placed her hands on Jasmine's shoulders as they descended. The stench wafting up to greet them was heavy with death and decay. Half way down they passed a small crawlspace, beyond which was a sanctum full of sarcophagi.

"It's getting hotter," noted Malika, wiping at a trickle of sweat running down her temple.

Eventually they came to a landing, and to their right was an entranceway, through which Jasmine saw the shadows shift on themselves.

Instinctively, she shot a protective hand in front of Malika.

The darkness roiled, forming tendrils of ectoplasm that curled across the floor like tentacles, only to shrink back again. They snaked away from a mass of gloom gathered in one corner of the small chamber like a ball of smoke, and as the ectoplasm parted in veils of black mist, Jasmine saw what lie beneath.

It was a woman, or had been once. Her heavy breasts sat flopped across an enormous belly, the decayed wedding dress damaged in spots to reveal bruised and veined flesh beneath, bluish-grey in hue. Her bloated face was similarly discoloured, the dusk of her eye-sockets contrasting sharply with her pale eyes, which sat in her face like hardboiled eggs. Big looped earrings of gold hung from her distended lobes, and a chain slung from one across her decomposing cheek to her flared nostrils, where it pierced the flesh without aid of a nose-ring.

The stench of death was in the air, and Jasmine could guess why: piles of bones lie heaped around the phantasm, the flesh sucked clean from them. The air was hot and humid, smothering the women as they stood aghast before the hideous woman.

"Christ, what is it?" said Jasmine quietly.

"This is the Jilted Bride of Darkness, a *djinn*,"

answered Malika, almost reverentially. "She
things."

The ectoplasm tendrils coiled out toward
so she shifted back a pace. The tendrils becam
the further they trailed from their source,
ones straying too far simply evaporated like s

"But she looks blind," whispered Jasmine.

"I am, but I hear well enough," said the Brid
voice hollow and mournful, sliding away
sentence to be replaced with another, slightly
in pitch. That, too, faded and was replaced wit
another voice, different again, each one layerin₂
other so it sounded to Jasmine as though se
people spoke at once, finishing each oth
sentences. "I am an augur," the djinn continued,
oracle. I can see into the darkness, see between
worlds and see clearly what you cannot. I can see
past, and the future. Which is it you seek?"

Jasmine could feel Malika trembling.

"The future," the old woman requested, shakin
with fear.

"Naturally, most do," said the Bride, her veils of
shadow billowing as they framed her grotesque face.

"No, more than that," Jasmine suddenly
announced, overtaken by inspiration. "I don't want to
know what the future is. I want to decide it."

The Bride laughed mirthlessly, the fat of her chin
wobbling.

"And you will, rat-woman. Near and far, you will.
Through blood and spirit our world will bend to
you."

"I don't want obedience," said Jasmine. "I only
want Raza."

The shadows roiled turbulently, and for a moment

Jasmine wondered if she had angered the djinn.

"The only way to get your husband is to fight for him," said the Bride.

"So he's alive then?" said Jasmine hopefully.

"He is."

A tear rolled down Jasmine's cheek. She'd been shielding herself from the potential news of his death, and now this phantasm who claimed to see futures was adamant he lived. It strengthened her resolve.

"Tell me how I get him back."

The darkness roiled again.

"You must give of yourself, rat-woman. These chuwa, it is not him they want, but you."

"Why?"

"For your blood," said the Bride.

The news wasn't at all what Jasmine could have guessed at. The thought that her blood was precious to these monsters was terrifying.

"There is a turf war happening, rat-woman, and the stakes are high," the Bride continued, sensing Jasmine's alarm. "These Chuwa can gain a considerable foothold on Lahore if they have you. But I warn you, they will have you for more than simply this, when they realise what you are."

"And what is she?" asked Malika, creasing her brows with concern.

"The Dark Star."

The phrase sounded familiar to Jasmine. She'd heard it before, but couldn't place where. Perhaps she'd only dreamt it? The Jilted Bride of Darkness had more bad news, however.

"If you leave our land, they will kill your husband. You must be willing. We have our own laws and covenants, and the chuwa cannot take you without your submission. But your husband is their property. They could take him whenever they wanted."

Jasmine couldn't help but glance at Malika, who looked away in shame. The old woman knew her crime, Jasmine reminded herself; there were bigger fish to fry here.

"Bride, is this why they did not take him on the times he returned here? Did they know he would eventually bring me here?"

The djinn's eyes rolled in their sockets, shining wetly.

"You ask what you already know," the Bride said with a hint of rebuke. "When they came for the baby, they saw the tickets for travel to a new land, did they not? The chuwa did consult me then, and I foresaw your coming through the passage of time, rat-woman. They have been waiting for you."

"You helped them?" Jasmine scoffed, screwing her nose up.

"I am neutral and take no sides," came the reply, the myriad voices overlapping. They were more discordant now, as though the longer she conferred, the less tangible her consultation. "I only see. But know this, rat-woman: I also see that you can free your husband, if you are strong. Succeed, Jasmine, and you can change our world forever."

There was a hint of warmth and promise to the phantasm's voice, bemusing Jasmine. She could have sworn it almost sounded as though the djinn *did* take sides, and had already decided which it would be.

The darkness before her wavered, and beyond the veils of shadow that roiled over the decayed body of the Bride, Jasmine glimpsed a core of flame, super-charged like a furnace. The shadows closed over again, the ectoplasm tendrils snaking out toward her feet. She let them touch her this time, watching as they playfully coiled over her feet. There was warmth to them; Jasmine suspected the fire she'd seen at the Bride's core had something to do with it.

"Thank you," she said with complete sincerity.

The tendrils withdrew, leaving her foot stained with soot.

"No gratitude necessary," said the Bride portentously. "Only payment."

There was an uneasy moment of silence, wherein the tension was so palpable Jasmine dared not move.

"Payment?" she ventured, the sweat stinging her eyes.

The whites of the djinn's eyes hadn't moved, but Jasmine felt they were trained solely on her.

"Of course," she stammered, reaching for her money.

"Something that means life to you," the djinn clarified.

Jasmine stayed her hand. Money wouldn't cut it, she realised. Then she saw the wedding band on her finger. A hole opened inside her at the thought of handing it over, as though she were giving away the very promise of love and unity she and Raza had promised one another. That meant life to her. Her fingers trembled as she tried to twist the ring free.

"No," said Malika, finding voice at last and closing her wrinkled hand over Jasmine's.

"But it's all I have, I swear," she said.

"There is something else you have," the Bride intoned. "Something I lost a long time ago. I will accept that."

Jasmine shook her head.

"I don't understand. I'm sorry, honestly..."

"You have life," said the Bride flatly.

The chamber echoed with her voice, and Jasmine stood shocked. This phantasm wanted her life? Had she not been fighting for just such a thing all along, and what of the djinn's prophecies? If Jasmine was dead, how would she do all these things the Jilted Bride of Darkness had only moments ago hinted at?

She turned to run but the ectoplasmic tendrils were quick, shooting across the space and twisting in the air before her, emitting a fierce heat. Behind her, the veils had shifted aside to reveal the red-hot kiln in the Bride's belly, a conflagration shimmering with such intensity the women had to shield their eyes from it. The roar of the furnace was loud in their ears.

"Please," begged Jasmine, tears springing to her eyes, "my husband... you said I could save him..."

Impassive, the djinn waited for payment.

"Jilted Bride."

It was Malika's voice, feeble against the roar of the Bride's fire.

The flames dimmed as the shadows closed over the Bride's belly.

"Will you accept me in her place?" said Malika.

Jasmine stared horrified at Raza's grandmother.

"Only if the beneficiary agrees," the voices from the roiling darkness said.

Malika regarded Jasmine sympathetically, stroking her hair. There was a resignation to the old woman's face.

"No, I won't agree to it," Jasmine said.

Malika's eyes were warm and loving, and for once Jasmine felt she saw the woman for who she truly was. There was no madness in her eyes, and no suffering.

"Jasmine-ji, my sweet granddaughter-in-law, you are so strong, so brave. Your love for my little Raza as brought you far, and changed you so much..."

The tears fell, from them both.

"Please stop," begged Jasmine.

"Standing beside you, I feel honoured and cleansed," Malika said with a sad smile. "There's good in you that infects those around you. Only you can save Raza now. There is only one currency the Bride deals in, and we have no sacrifice here."

The tendrils snaked across the floor, eager for their claim. Jasmine felt sickened by their hunger.

"You could have brought something," she said to Malika, without accusation. "An animal maybe, like the ones for Eid."

"Shush, child. It doesn't work like that. Use this goodness in you, defeat these monsters. You go–"

"No," sobbed Jasmine as her grandmother-in-law disengaged from their embrace.

"You go and you take back your husband."

Jasmine stood shaking her head, trembling with grief. The way Raza's grandmother accepted her destiny gracefully, though it meant certain death, broke Jasmine's heart. Malika was sacrificing herself, and for what? What had the Bride truly given her, besides clarity? The hard work was still left for her, which made the price to pay seem unbalanced.

Malika approached her one final time, taking Jasmine's head in her steady hands and lowering it to kiss the top of her head. Jasmine sniffed as she wiped at the tears on her cheeks.

"This is the only way," Malika whispered, before turning to face the Bride.

"You are free to leave, rat-woman," the Bride intoned. "Take it."

The ectoplasm strands darted across the floor, circling Malika's feet, spiralling quickly up her legs. Malika paid them no heed, glancing back at Jasmine over her shoulder with a dazzling smile. She seemed to Jasmine to be the most beautiful woman in the world, her strength and selflessness outshining the burning core of the Jilted Bride beyond her.

Jasmine couldn't bear to watch, and fled up the stairwell just as a bright light shone from the chamber below. She crawled the last of the stairs and threw herself onto the floor of the mausoleum, screaming in anguish. The thought of leaving Malika alone down there with that phantasm, knowing it meant the old woman's death, sent her mind reeling. She wished to sprint down and rip the djinn apart with her claws, but even she had sensed the magnificent power that resided within the Jilted Bride of Darkness. It would be a futile effort which would certainly doom Raza.

She'd been given a chance; Malika had bought her that much with her sacrifice.

A movement on the ceiling caught her attention, her head snapping back to assess the threat.

Their bodies as pale as ivory, their eyes cold and lifeless, the self-proclaimed angels clung precariously to the vaulted ceiling, regarding her dispassionately. Munkar and Nakir.

Jasmine assumed a fighting stance, claws extended and teeth bared. But her newly-tuned intuition told her they weren't here for her. The angels crawled spider-like across the ceiling toward the wall she'd passed through.

"Be kind to her," implored Jasmine. "She was a

good woman."

"We know," said Nakir in that hissing voice they shared.

Jasmine glowered at them as she crept backwards toward the sunshine outside. The angels paused at the opening, watching her.

"We'll be back for you soon enough, chuwa," promised Munkar.

They slunk through the hole in the wall and down into the dark recess of the stairwell.

Jasmine faced the day, taking comfort in the sun beating down on a field of dry grass. It wasn't much to look at, but it wasn't monstrous, at least. She'd had her fill of the latter for one day, though it was far from over.

The sound of stones sliding into place against one another made her look around, and she saw the wall was whole again, a little puff of dust dissipating in the air as though the bricks had slammed together quickly. The entrance to the Bride was gone, as was her bloody hand print, it having dried and flaked off when the wall originally dissolved.

As she made her way back along the brick passageway to the road, she allowed herself to cry for Malika one last time, and then she had to save her strength for the trials ahead. The Bride might have said she would succeed, but she hadn't said it would be easy. She hadn't needed to; Jasmine already knew it would be one of the most trying times of her life.

When she reached the steel gate she'd broken open earlier, where Imran snored loudly inside his auto-rickshaw, Jasmine heard the songbirds chirruping in the trees around her. Even they knew the tomb and its surrounds was a place of death, and avoided it.

CHAPTER 21

The *goree* hadn't looked too pleased when she'd returned from the tomb, and had insisted that the old woman they'd brought with them wouldn't be joining them, so it was with reluctance that Imran informed his troubled passenger that they had company.

"What do you mean?" Jasmine said, immediately spinning in her seat to pull at the canvas flap behind her, spying through the hole she made with her claws.

Following like a shark was a black sedan, but what really made it stand out from the crowd was how clean it was. Its black finish had been polished with such gusto there was no layer of dust on its roof or bonnet, unlike the vehicles around it.

"*Goondas*," said Imran, watching them in his side mirrors. "Mafia mens. Hold on to the tights, Mrs Jasmine!"

He accelerated the rickshaw to its fullest, the little engine coughing and spluttering before launching them into the traffic ahead, Imran yanking the steering wheel as he veered through narrow spaces between cars. The black sedan glided effortlessly abreast of them, gradually edging them off the road. Imran slammed on the brakes, putting his rickshaw behind the car, then throttled full-hilt, guiding the rickshaw into a U-turn and into oncoming traffic. The ploy worked momentarily, gaining them the advantage of distance.

The *goondas* waved their guns at the other drivers until they'd cleared a route into the other lane, moving into the slipstream parallel to the rickshaw. Soon the sedan had closed the distance again, as Imran fought against the incoming traffic on his side of the road.

The window of the sedan lowered, and Jasmine recognised the man who leaned out from it. It was Ahmad, the bastard who'd murdered the beggar-woman at Shahi Mohalla. In his hand was a pistol and he aimed it now at Imran, demanding the rickshaw-wallah pull over.

"He wanting me to stop, Mrs Jasmine," said Imran, stating the obvious. "But for you, I will not. Instead I will give him the smoke for eating."

"Good idea," said Jasmine, nodding. "We're both dead if you stop."

The little two-stroke engine revved unsteadily as the rickshaw struggled to outrun the sedan.

"Imran!" shouted Jasmine.

Ahmad grinned as he steadied the point of the gun at the rickshaw-wallah. He made a wave goodbye gesture.

The rickshaw suddenly banked to the left, away from the mafia men, and straight through a crowd of people, the horn squawking under Imran's fist. People fled in all directions as Imran drove the rickshaw straight up a narrow street. The walls either side began to close in.

Jasmine looked behind and saw the sedan inching

its way from one side of the road to the other, causing chaos as it tried to give chase. Gunshots fired into the air helped lubricate the wheels of charity, the crowds parting quickly so the vehicle had right of way and was careering toward the little auto-rickshaw.

"What the hell are you doing?" bellowed Jasmine, eyes wild. "Now we're trapped!"

All around them were pop-up market stalls full of chopped bananas or skinned chickens, flies buzzing arbitrarily over everything. Small boys splashed with ink stared out from the doorways of printing presses, crammed side-by-side with yet more businesses full of brightly-coloured cloth or bottles on tincture and medicines. There were sour looks and cursed words as stall operators pulled their tables back to allow the rickshaw to squeeze past. A man appeared before them, waving them forward and holding the press of people to one side. It became a group effort, and Jasmine marvelled at how they were able to continue driving through what looked to her like nothing more than a pedestrian access.

"We is not stuck," chuckled Imran. "But they is."

The sedan had reached its limit, and was currently being told so by a small crowd of men gathered at the driver's window. There was absolutely no room for the large vehicle to follow.

A surviving part of the old rampart which once surrounded the Walled City rose on their right, which put them deep within the confines of the old part of the city. The rickshaw was rolling along at a slow crawl by now, pedestrians passing it by. When they took a peek at the passenger in back, Jasmine heard some whisper *chuwa*. She pulled her *dupatta* closer to better conceal her face.

"We'd be better going by foot, wouldn't we?" she said.

Imran was abundantly optimistic. He poked his head out the side and peered ahead.

"We can go more, maybe fifty percent more," he said cheerily.

Behind them, Ahmad and his goons had forsaken their vehicle and were pushing through the crowds, waving their AK-47s in the air to procure an easier route.

"No, we need to go now," said Jasmine, climbing out of the rickshaw.

Imran craned his neck out the side and saw the *goondas* gaining ground.

"*Aacha,* no problem," he agreed, alarmed, and followed.

Jasmine shoved through the press of people, ignoring those who stared open-mouthed.

"Listen, Imran, we need to split up. You go that way, and I'll go this way."

The rickshaw-wallah looked uncertain.

"But Mrs Jasmine, you will be getting lost, *na?*"

He peered around, noting the various lanes snaking away in all directions, their canopies low and blocking the light of day.

Jasmine grinned at him.

"We have a saying in Australia: I'm going to make like a rat up a drain-pipe."

She reached up and tugged her *dupatta* off, letting her blonde tresses fall down to her shoulders, exposed for the crowd around them to see. A stray shaft a sunbeam lit her hair up like a beacon, dazzling the onlookers. There were gasps and murmurs of a chuwa in their midst, as Jasmine slowly pirouetted to reveal the changes wrought upon her face. A swell of people closest to her fell back in fear, knocking over people behind them. There was moment's domino effect, which ended when a stand of betelnuts toppled over, the nuts rolling underfoot and causing more mayhem.

Imran was baffled, but Jasmine shoved him backwards, imploring him to run. The rickshaw-wallah took to his heels, slipping easily into the pressing throng. It occurred to Jasmine the man could have easily disappeared anytime he'd wanted, but he'd stuck by her side where she had fumbled with navigating the crush of people.

From back towards the main street, she could see the mafia men on tip-toe studying the fracas that had exploded around her. She saw Ahmad pointing in her direction.

As she made her way to the nearest wall, the crowd moved away as though propelled by a magnetic force. Jasmine knew the *goondas* couldn't help but notice the effect on the crowd ahead of them. The wall was solid concrete, but old. Cracks and lichen defaced it. The downpipe hadn't fared much better since when it had been screwed into the cement. She gave it a little shake, testing its ability to hold weight. Promising, but not altogether reassuring.

The *goondas* were nearly upon her now, readying their weapons.

Jasmine took hold of the drainpipe and began to climb, using the claws on her toes and hands to aid her. They dug into the ancient cement easily, propelling her upwards in parody of her rock-climbing experience. At three stories the cement rendering had ceased, and only exposed ancient brick remained for the subsequent two stories. This made the climb simpler, her claws finding purchase easier than on the relatively smooth concrete further below.

A knife ricocheted off the brickwork beside her, sending chips and dust into her face.

"Careful, careful," she heard Ahmad caution his men down below. "Don't hit her vital organs."

She lifted her elbow to peek down at her pursuers, just in time to see Ahmad's men through a doorway in the building. One remained in the bazaar, his Kalashnikov pointed in her direction.

She was nearly at the top now. She pulled herself the remainder of the distance and the drainpipe's hold on the wall gave way, shrieking as the metal buckled under her weight. She scrambled for purchase, her claws digging into the masonry as her lifeline fell away. The drainpipe fell horizontally into the air behind her, striking the wall on the opposite building and lodging like a fragile bridge between the two. As tempting as it was to cross to the other building, Jasmine knew she was too heavy for the drainpipe.

She heaved herself up and over the edge of the building, her foot dislodging an old brick on the eave. She heard it crash into a pile of brassware down in the market, and hoped the *goonda* had been felled by it as well.

The rooftop was blessedly free of people. The only thing up here was a pigeon coop, the birds fussing over one another and preening their feathers. She looked out across the Walled City. It stretched far and wide, and for the first time she had a sense of how impressive and densely packed it was, how from it the entire city of Lahore had emerged, spreading out in all directions. But this was the city's heart, there was no doubt: it throbbed with life day and night, shaped by the human drama contained in its radius, the triumphs and the losses all.

Across the lanes on the other rooftops there was life: young boys flew kites, teasing the strings to entice their charges to spin and whirl in the skies above the old city. Washer-women hung clothes, tucking the corners of the laundry between the twists between two ropes without aid of pegs. Several buildings away an old man sat smoking, admiring the view. He looked at peace. It was a different world up here above the maze of chaotic markets and diesel-choked corridors.

From a darkened door of the stairway bulkhead burst the *goondas*, led by Ahmad. They blinked furiously against the sunlight, having grown accustomed to the dark of the stairs in their short sojourn from the bazaar.

"Shit!" cried Jasmine, and following with a snarl she struck at the man nearest to her, knocking the gun from his hand.

She stepped in and punched him square in the chest, toppling him backwards, in reach of his dropped weapon.

Ahmad closed the distance and brought his pistol down on the back of her head. She staggered from his blow, and had she have still been entirely human, she was sure she'd be unconscious on the floor. As the other two *goondas* rushed her, she backhanded Ahmad across the face before she was tackled to the ground.

They were on top of her now, holding her down,

and the *goonda* sitting on her chest drove his fist down into her face. She tasted blood, and cement dust. With a guttural growl she heaved the *goondas* off, flipping onto her feet. A gun was pointed at her so she simply snatched it from the man and tossed it over the edge of the roof. Now she had the man in her vice-like grip, her claws digging into the muscle of his arms. The sound from her throat was bestial, and the look in her eyes was hunger, as she opened her maw slowly and pulled the man closer. He struggled to keep his head from her jaws, her spittle flecking him.

She lifted the man into the air and threw him into the space beyond the roof edge. He fell with a scream, followed by the crashing of the drainpipe being knocked from its precarious bridging, silenced only when his body hit the street below.

Her arm stung, and a knife clattered to the concrete in front of her. She glanced down to see the *kameez* torn where the blade had sliced through both fabric and flesh. Blood beaded at the wound. She spun on her heel to see the *goonda* who'd thrown the knife, and behind him, Ahmad aiming his pistol in her direction. If he fired, the bullet would find its mark where the knife hadn't, she was sure.

The edge of the roof was about five feet away. She sprinted for it, her calves like suspension springs, launching her across the short stretch between buildings and landing her effortlessly onto the roof of the neighbouring edifice.

At Ahmad's command his goons took a run-up, weapons slung across their backs, leaping across the distance to take chase.

Jasmine dashed to the opposite border, leaping

effortlessly across to the next rooftop. A washer-woman flapped a wet bed-sheet at her, shock and revulsion etched on the woman's face. A flock of chickens at her feet squawked loudly, scattering from her.

The pursuit continued across several more buildings, their proximity permitting the *goondas* easy-enough chase.

Ahmad threatened the washerwomen with his gun, waving it in their faces. Jasmine could see the sense of power he took in frightening the women. It made Jasmine's blood boil.

A bullet struck the bulkhead behind her, frightening the boys with the kites on the next rooftop over, and reminding her to keep moving. She may have put distance between herself and the mafia men, but they were relentless and armed. They might still only be human, but that made them all the more dangerous. She hoped the gunshot was enough to alert the rooftop community to the danger they were in if they lingered. With some relief she saw the boys flee for their stairwell, their abandoned kites drifting aimlessly across the Walled City.

A cry behind her caught her attention, and she turned in time to see one of the *goondas* strike the eave as he leapt, his hands madly scrambling for purchase and failing. He disappeared over the side. Ahmad stared down into the space where his man had fallen; jogging back, he took a run-up and cleared the expanse.

Jasmine bolted behind a bulkhead when an arm shot out from the doorway of an annex, catching her throat and dropping her to the floor. She was winded, struggling for air. From the annex stepped the *goonda* who had stayed below in the marketplace when the others had ascended in pursuit. He pointed his Kalashnikov at her chest. Jasmine rolled over to crawl away, but the goon planted a foot in the small of her back, pinning her to the cool concrete.

"You heathen monster," he snarled. "They want you alive, but shit like you is better off dead."

She felt the hard tip of his gun pressed to the back of her skull.

"No," she gasped, thinking only she had failed Raza.

A gunshot echoed off the buildings, ringing in her ears.

The body of the *goonda* dropped beside her, his head bouncing off the floor. In the centre of his forehead was a hole, from which blood trickled.

Straining her neck, she saw Ahmad standing atop the eave of the neighbouring building, the smoking pistol in his hand.

"She is to be taken alive, you idiot!" the mafia man yelled to his dead companion.

Jasmine turned over and kicked her feet, shuffling backwards as Ahmad readied himself for the final jump. The door inside the annex was the obvious escape route, but it lead to an entire marketplace full of people, who though hadn't been too alarmed at the sight of the AK-47s (after all, every bank and McDonald's had guards brandishing the weapons so it was hardly an anomaly here), would be in danger were the mafia men to open fire on her down below. She had to keep the chase on the rooftops, but she struggled to regain her breath and even now Ahmad was leaping across the space to where she sat.

Beside her was a spool of thread, a light powder

dusted on its twine. It gave her an idea.

Ahmad stalked across the rooftop, certain the chase was over. He'd seen the rat-woman winded, and knew that despite her supernatural strength she would tire soon.

"I know you're here, chuwa," he said calmly, relishing the moment. "I can smell your sweat; smell your fear."

He spied her sleeve at the corner of the bulkhead, and rushed forward, warning her not to move lest she get a bullet in the legs. To his immense satisfaction, the rat-woman with the golden hair stood there, back to the wall, panting from exertion. He'd thought perhaps she'd designed a trap for him, tearing the sleeve of her *kameez* off to hang on a nail.

"It's all over now, *gora gora,*" he taunted. "You're now the bargaining chip of the Lakar Baga Badmash, so turn around slowly with your hands behind you."

The gun waved at her, so Jasmine did as she was instructed, and held her hands behind her back. Ahmad lowered the weapon long enough to pull a pair of clunky wrist-cuffs from a utility belt beneath his *kameez,* but it was all the time Jasmine needed. She bolted for the edge of the roof and was across the divide and onto the next rooftop in a low crouch while Ahmad fumbled with the cuffs and pistol. He took up the chase anew, cursing at having been tricked into thinking the foreigner was too exhausted to keep running.

As he sailed across the gap he noticed the rat-woman had given up her flight, and was standing at the far end of the rooftop watching him expectantly. Too late did he see the kite-string stretched across the edge of the eave at head-height. The diamond dust glinted in the sunlight, slicing his throat clean open as he made the landing. The string snapped, coiling around his neck as he stumbled and fell to his knees, a geyser of blood spraying up from the side of his throat.

Jasmine watched impassively. The man deserved it, as far as she was concerned. She had avenged the death of the beggar-woman. As she turned to leave, she was startled to see a small girl standing at the top of the stairs inside the bulkhead. The girl was frozen to the spot, and when Jasmine smiled at her, the girl erupted into a scream of horror.

Jasmine's hand reflexively reached for her own face, and feeling the changes – her nose and lips more animal, a light down of fur sprouting across her cheeks and forehead – she snatched her hand away fearfully and stared at the claws on the ends of her fingers. She was a monster, no doubt about it.

The young girl fled down the stairwell, and shouts of alarm arose from inside. She distinctly heard them mention a chuwa. It was time to go.

The bleached domes of the Badshahi Mosque rose beautifully beyond the perimeter of the Walled City to her left, so it was in that direction Jasmine began to leap from rooftop to rooftop, careful to avoid anyone who might be enjoying the solitude of life above the bazaars. She knew her mission now, and there'd be no turning back on it.

CHAPTER 22

The hallways of the Mohallan warren were vacant, the rat-people having bedded down in their nests. The chuwa needed only a few hours rest at a time, and would soon rise to tend to their daily chores again. But not all had retired; from down the corridor came voices in heated discussion.

"We must rein this *gora* woman in," said Aru-Min, clenching his fists in frustration. "She will bring disaster upon us."

He faced against Dhama and Velli, flanked by Nagal sat on the steps of the brick podium behind, nodding in agreement.

"Word is that the woman has taken matters into her own hands," said Nagal. "She is out of her depth, Dhama."

The wizened chuwa scratched at his beard thoughtfully, his lids heavy with the burden of decision. His tribe had been vexed by the events unfolding in their city, and were understandably worried. Never before had a foreigner been initiated into their way of life, and the chaos which had consequently ensued couldn't be ignored.

"The Jamallans won't touch her," said Velli. "They still observe the covenant."

There was a sharp laugh from Nagal.

"There are other things besides our wayward brother beneath Shah Jamal, Velli. And not all of

222

those things recognise covenants."

"The Jamal sect wants her to work for them, we already know this," said Aru-Min, his stone bracelets flashing with reflected candlelight as he waved his hands in the air. "They want to control Lahore; we know this, too. Yet, she runs around out there looking for so-called answers while we do nothing? We can only blame ourselves when the trouble is too great to manage."

Velli shook her head disagreeably. She was about to voice a rebuke when another voice silenced her.

"Take me to them," demanded Jasmine from the archway.

Dhama turned to face her, noting the torn and bloodied *shalwar-kameez* she wore. It made him think of how he endeavoured for his tribe to assimilate with the humans aboveground, to adopt their ways and culture and perhaps, one day, be accepted, to live in harmony with the human race. Perhaps he needn't worry too much about the white woman's allegiances when it came to Mohallans and Jamallans, he mused.

"I know what I must do," the woman insisted.

Dhama approached her.

"And what is that? Go to them, so they can take you?"

Jasmine nodded, even as Velli protested.

"You are safe while you avoid them," said Velli. "They cannot break the covenant."

There was a hard glint in the white woman's eyes.

"Raza's grandmother gave herself to the Bride of Darkness, so I may be free. And now I must give myself to them, that Raza may be free."

Dhama sighed.

"You risk everything, Jasmine. They want you for

some greater purpose we do not yet understand. Don't do this thing."

She continued to stare resolutely at him. He knew the look well; it was same belligerence he had to counter in Kha'i every time he faced off with the Jamallan.

"Take me," she demanded again.

Dhama clenched his teeth.

"Then let the deaths of many be on *your* hands only," he said, beckoning her to follow.

Under cover of darkness, Dhama led a contingent of chuwa from the Mohalla warren and up into the laneways of the Walled City, their faces covered by scarves. His tribe had been visibly shaken by Jasmine's presence when they'd awoken, following rumours which had spread like wildfire throughout the supernatural community. She had scolded the angel soul-suckers with the fires of Hell itself, some said; the legendary Jilted Bride of Darkness had feared for her own life when lasers had shot from the foreign rat-woman's eyes, yet others whispered. Dhama knew better than to put his faith in such tales.

A brightly coloured truck festooned with brass bells was waiting for them close to the entrance of the Walled City, outside Taxali Gate. The truck driver leaned out his window as the troupe passed, and Dhama stopped to shake the man's hand.

"Your kindnesses are always remembered by us,

my friend," said Dhama warmly. "Anything your family needs, Sameer, you let us know."

"This is my honour, and my duty," the truck-driver gushed. "Please, you embarrass me."

His eyes lingered on Jasmine as she passed.

"Times are changing," Dhama said, noting the man's interest. "The old ways are just that: old."

The truck driver waggled his head, holding his hand over his heart. Dhama smiled and joined his tribe in the rear of the truck, pulling a canvas flap down for privacy. Aru-Min banged on the steel walls three times, and the vehicle lurched, crawling along until it merged with the traffic on Circular Road.

The chuwa were silent on the journey, each regarding Jasmine with mixed emotions. She didn't care; their companionship was irrelevant. She had already sacrificed her humanity to these creatures in her bid to rescue Raza; if she had to lay down the law, so to speak, to continue those efforts, then so be it. If the chuwa didn't like, then stiff shit, Jasmine figured.

Eventually the truck squealed to a stop, and when Jasmine flung the canvas flap aside she was met with an explosion of light and noise. It was as though a nightclub had refused to be contained by four walls and had spilled into the open.

"This is Shah Jamal?" she asked of Dhama, and he confirmed it was.

She had expected a sombre crypt hidden by creepy mist, wherein Kha'i and his followers would be lurking. Instead, there was a crumbling lichen-covered wall from which grew ferns, beyond which was an expansive courtyard filled with revellers, all young men. They cheered on a small posse of much older men who whirled like dervishes, their scraggly long hair and beards lifting into the air with the motion of their dancing. Behind the dancers sat two additional men, beating on the skins of large drums. They were topless, these musicians, sweat pouring down their muscled torsos as they beat out a tattoo.

Rising above this tableau were massive ficus trees, backlit by spotlights, their branches spread out so far they reached over the road where the chuwa now assembled. Sameer drove away to park the truck further down the road, away from the obstruction of cars and motorbikes positioned on the street closest to the party.

"This is Shahi Jamal," said Velli, at Jasmine's shoulder. There was a note of distaste in the rat-woman's tone. "The tomb of the Sufi saint is up there."

Jasmine followed to where Velli pointed, and could see that beyond the canopy of the trees there was a small brick edifice atop an imposing wall behind the crowd and dancers. To the right of the ficus trees were a set of stone stairs, congested by young men clamouring to reach the top, some as pissed as rats on bootleg alcohol judging by their heavy eyelids and lopsided grins.

"Follow," Dhama said simply, leading his tribe across the dusty street.

It was late dusk by now, and the headlamps of the cars creeping past the site of the tomb pierced the plumes of dust to pick out the details of the public. The chuwa kept their scarves and *dupattas* bound tightly over their faces, their black eyes shining wetly from the space between the folds. They weren't the only ones with coverings, fortunately: many of the patrons yet to enter had pulled their shirts or scarves over their faces to stop from inhaling the dust the traffic kicked up. The chuwa blended in well on that score.

The noise of the proceedings intensified once inside the walls, the air electric with danger and delusion. To their immediate right, outside a row of toilet cubicles, a makeshift drug laboratory had been set up, gas burners set down on the concrete floor with pots boiling above them.

"Soma," sneered Velli. "Low potency, but more than capable for these humans."

Jasmine was about to ask what precisely it was capable of, when she saw a gang of young men exchange money for a serving of the broth. They gathered excitedly around it, spooning a serving each into their mouths. Her keen eyesight could easily see their pupils dilate, the blood pulse through their temples as the veins on their necks stood out. A faint, greenish glow infused their irises.

"It's a drug?" asked Jasmine.

Velli nodded, following Dhama to the base of the stairs. There was no way they'd reach the top, Jasmine knew: it was too crowded, and those who stood on the steps were unable to move for the ones before them. It was a gridlock, and many had simply decided to enjoy a birds-eye view through the ficus canopy of the festivities in the neighbouring courtyard.

Dhama reached up and slid back his scarf, his huge hairy ears springing loose, his wild white hair waving in the air. The young men before him were alarmed by the sight of him, struggling to edge away from the old rat-man. They mouthed surprise, shoving desperately at the crowd above. When they failed to gain distance, they simply leapt from the steps to the ground, fleeing to the street behind the chuwa troupe.

The rest of the rat-people followed suit, unmasking themselves to the horror of the crowd around them. There were some – those young men who had consumed the soma – who reached out to touch the chuwa, for blessings perhaps, or to boast to family and friends that they'd touched the dangerously divine and lived to tell the tale. But for most of the gathering their superstitious natures held fast, and so when Dhama began a slow ascent up the steps, the young men followed the example of their brothers and climbed down the side of the stone staircase. Those at the top, seeing what advanced toward them, held their breaths and used the newfound empty space of the stairs to spread themselves thin, creating a corridor through the crowd for the venerated chuwa.

Jasmine could see many of the young men had the same tell-tale greenish glow in their eyes, however faint it was.

At the summit there was less room than below, a sizeable crowd standing shoulder-to-shoulder to admire a performance of dancers pogo'ing to the beat of a *dholi*. Again, room was made for the chuwa, the audience nearly tripping over themselves as they took to the staircase, filling the void behind the procession of rat-people.

"These dancers are Sufis, kind of like living saints," explained Velli of the topless man leaping up and down. To their left were three marble sarcophagi behind chain-link wire. "Those are the dead ones."

Dhama cleared a path to the front, where the more

affluent of society sat on cushions to enjoy the performance. Upon seeing the wizened chuwa, these people quickly proffered their prime seating, themselves scuttling back into the press of dusty young men at their backs, reduced to nothing more than another lowly spectator.

But Dhama had no interest in Sufi dancers and their *dholis*: he pressed his hand to his heart as a sign of gratitude and respect, and continued to trek past the performance – the dancer in such a transcendental state he was unaware of the presence of the rat-people – guiding his tribe through the underbrush beside the scarp of rock beyond. The chuwa dipped their heads beneath the low-hanging braches, marching on until Dhama indicated they'd reached their destination. The light and noise of the festivities of Shah Jamal filtered through the copse of jungle to them.

"Is this it?" said Jasmine, inspecting the rocky face of the escarpment.

As if in answer to her query, a rat-woman in an olive-green dress with elaborate tattoos inked across her shaved skull appeared from the rock. It was as though she simply materialised before it. Only when the woman stepped forward, sharing the same patch of soil as the Mohallans, did Jasmine understand the deception. It was trick of the eye: there was an open cave in the rock which directed to a dog-leg corridor, and the rocky wall of the corridor served to appear as part of the escarpment face.

"Everyone is fooled by it," she heard Velli smiling behind her. "It protects this entrance from trespassers. When The Host doesn't."

The one Velli called The Host – the new arrival with the tattoos – regarded them all with open hostility.

Dhama cleared his throat.

"We seek an audience with the Jamallans," he said. "The girl wishes to speak with Kha'i."

The Host couldn't help but smile triumphantly.

"Very well, follow me."

The Host retraced her steps, re-entering the illusion and disappearing around the corner of the dog-leg, descending a stairwell hidden in the gloom.

Dhama turned to Jasmine.

"I really hope you know what you're doing."

"Me, too," she replied grimly.

Dhama lowered his eyes, scratching at his chin.

"Stay close to me at all times," he said, for her benefit only.

He guided the Mohallan tribe of chuwa into the inky maw of the escarpment, the beat of the drums vibrating through the rock like a quickened heartbeat, in time with Jasmine's own. She took a deep breath and followed the rat-people down the hole.

CHAPTER 23

Beneath Shah Jamal were offshoot corridors along the cave they'd entered through – the walls of which were ancient Harappan brick, Velli explained – which led to various rooms and chambers, each serving some recognisable purpose: kitchen, laundry, nursery. There were others, too, slightly more arcane: an armourer, an iron-smith, an alchemist. Necessities of an army, not a benevolent community. The one thing they held in common was they stank of urine, as the Mohallan sanctuary had. Jasmine began to differentiate between the different scents of the urine; each invested with particular significance, she supposed. Wooden torches aflame in their brackets lit the way, and as Jasmine passed a darkened hall to her left she distinctly heard her name whispered.

She halted, listening intently for the source. She tried to see into the darkness of a breakaway cavern, but even her chuwa eyes weren't yet up to the task. She considered calling out to Dhama and the rest of the chuwa, to let them know there was something in need of investigation, but the old rat had proven just as much a hindrance to her search for Raza as anyone, so she kept her tongue.

The sound came again, urgent, calling her name.

She slipped into the side cavern, plunging

headlong into its dark mystery, running her fingertips along the walls to feel her way.

"Raza?" she hoarsely whispered. "Is that you?"

The gloom gave way ahead to the flickering light of a torch on the wall. It lit a chamber at the end of the cavern, along the wall of which were set iron bars. It was clearly a prison, and behind the bars sat the prisoners, chuwa in various stages of development, their transformation from human to rat diverging into disasters, malformations growing from their heads or backs. They were pitiful things, thin and starved, moaning for assistance when they saw her.

Jasmine was horrified by the state of them. It seemed to her that too easily could her own infected bite have sent her down their miserable path, deforming her beyond the human visage she still (thankfully) wore beneath the fur and fangs.

"Raza," she whispered again, eagerly searching the gaunt faces staring back.

He wasn't in there. She stepped back to take stock of the tragedy before her, wondering how she might free the captives, when she bumped into something behind that didn't feel like rock or brick. It was warm, and furry.

Even as she leapt aside, the wall behind her unfurled, as a millipede might, expanding into the room. Incisors the length of her entire arm gnashed at the air before her face, so large and sharp they'd have easily taken her head off.

Arms from behind seized her, pulling her backwards until she was slammed against the iron bars. The captives had reached through the bars to pin her against the cell doors. She struggled against their clutches, but though weak they were many.

"Let go!" she demanded, vainly.

The beast before her had risen to its full height, revealing itself to be a goliath rat taller than she, its girth easily that of a large car. There was nothing human about it – it was a hundred percent animal, albeit hideously out of proportion to the size of its species. The way it squatted down on its haunches told Jasmine it was ready to launch into attack.

"Let me go!" she cried, struggling to free her arms and legs from the prisoners' hold.

The monster lunged at her, ready to devour her or tear her limb from limb.

Its teeth snapped a foot from her face, foetid breath making her dry-heave. But that was as far as the monster advanced, and when she heard the chain rattle against the wall behind it, Jasmine nearly laughed. This was the confrontation with the Arms Bearer at the foot of the Mohallan sect's stairs all over again. The rat-monster roared, spittle flecking Jasmine's face and hair. She turned her head aside and clenched her eyes shut, expecting the chain to give way and the monster to be upon her, but the chain held tight.

"Go now," whispered a voice close to her ear.

Jasmine opened her eyes and saw a face pressed against the bars just inches from her own. It was a woman, though her features had long since morphed into something nightmarish, with one eye twice the size of the other and a row of teeth growing through the skin of a cheek. Bushels of fur bloomed in random patches across her face.

Unable to reach her, the rat-monster snorted in frustration and shook its body, rattling the chain slung from its neck to the heavy-duty bracket on the far wall. Piles of bones – human, or near enough – lay scattered on the floor below it, remains of trespassers whom the goliath had devoured.

Jasmine realised the prisoners had saved her life: had they not hauled her against the cell doors, the rat-monster would certainly have pounced upon her.

"We will help you," croaked another, a man as far as Jasmine could discern. A fat tail hung from his rear, and his back was bent and spiny. Stretched skin shone where new bones were trying to force their way out from within his body.

"Let me help you," said Jasmine. "I can free you."

"There's no time, or means," the woman said.

Jasmine studied the doors and the locks, and knew it to be true. They were built to withstand the strength of a chuwa, and made to contain a dozen more. Her newborn strength would be insufficient.

"Your love he is near," the woman said, sniffing at the air.

Holding her against the bars still, the captives inched Jasmine along toward the entranceway, ensuring no part of her strayed from against the bars lest the goliath charge across the room and haul Jasmine to her death. The rat-monster followed her progress, testing the limits of the chains' reach several times. Eventually she reached the safety of the cavern entrance, and the prisoners released her. The goliath, cognizant it had been outdone, retreated to its nest amongst the bones, glaring balefully at the prisoners in their cells.

"I'll come back for you, I promise," said Jasmine, waving her gratitude to the captives before retreating back along the gloomy corridor.

Half way along she was met by The Host, the rat-woman standing still as a statue. She was expression-less as Jasmine passed by wordlessly, and only when they'd both returned to the cavern with the torches they'd first traversed did The Host have something to say of Jasmine's truancy.

"You'd do well to stay close to me, this time. Dhama isn't here, and you're on Jamallan turf now."

Jasmine held her tongue, and went ahead of The Host, following the light of the torches until they reached what The Host called The Elucidation Chamber, stinking no less of urine than the other rooms she'd passed had. When she sniffed at the air, Jasmine had the impression this was a room where the deepest political decisions were made. As if to further advance this notion, the centre of the room had a mandala painted on the floor, concentric rings following a channel carved into the stone. At the centre was a dais, with a symbol painted atop – it reminded Jasmine of the Arms Bearer symbol of the door of the Mohallan chuwa's home. There were rings cut into the walls, too, circling the entire chamber and crossing through niches, wherein were stuffed the mortal remains of holy men past. They were arranged in a standing position, dressed in fineries so new it could only have been Kha'i and his people who tended to them.

"Speak of the devil," said Jasmine under her breath as the Jamallan leader stalked into the chamber, followed by his coterie.

She knew it was he, for everyone in the room, including The Host herself, were in deference to the rat-man. That and her finely-tuned olfactory senses read the urine markings in the chamber, and her brain translated it to mean Kha'i held dominion here.

A scurry of activity and squeaking announced the arrival of hundreds of rats, darting from holes close to the ceiling and running along a carved shelf of stone until they'd circled the entire room and sat shoulder-to-shoulder, staring down at proceedings with beady black eyes.

From another doorway emerged Dhama and the Mohallan chuwa, and when he saw her he shook his head softly, as if to admonish her for sneaking off earlier. Aru-Min was smirking when she made eye-contact with him, so she refocused her attentions on Kha'i. He was younger than the Mohallan leader, slender with a robust chest and long neck. His black eyes were narrowed in eternal suspicion, beneath arched brows. His jet-black hair was tied up in a ponytail on the back of his head, Samurai-style. He was immaculately presented, right down to his polished claws, in complete contrast to Dhama's dishevelled, earthy demeanour.

"So, you're the *goree* causing everyone so much trouble?" he snickered.

"That's the one the Bride predicted," one of his tribe piped up, a rat-man with vitiligo covering half his head. Jasmine recognised this one: he'd been present at Raza's kidnapping.

"Oh, do shut up, Pirak," sniped Kha'i, to a round of tittering from the Jamallan chuwa.

The rat-man with the pale blotches on his face scowled, but kept his tongue.

An attendant chuwa appeared beside Kha'i, holding a bowl of viscous liquid. When the rat-man dipped in his fingers knuckle-deep and sucked the juices off, his eyes took on a greenish hue, as though they glowed radioactively. Jasmine figured this must be the soma she'd seen the young men partaking of in the celebrations above-ground, thought its effect on Kha'i was tenfold. So bright were his eyes Jasmine wondered how it was possible he was even able to see.

A monkey snuck in from the corridor behind her, quickly climbing the wall and jostling for position amongst the rats. They hissed and bared their incisors, but the monkey persisted and was rewarded with a prime position. Jasmine stared accusingly at it, for she supposed the simian was part of Iqbal, the Monkey-Man. Either he was locked up somewhere and curious to watch proceedings, or he felt too ashamed to come and witness in person. Jasmine hoped it was both, actually. The monkey wouldn't meet her eyes, deliberately watching her from its periphery only.

When the burning emerald in Kha'i's eyes dissipated, Dhama stepped forward from the throng of Mohallan chuwa.

"Let's get on with this, Kha'i."

"Was it you who proposed this meeting, Dhama?" snarled Kha'i. "No? Then hold your tongue. It was she–"

The Jamallan leader pointed a bony finger in Jasmine's direction.

"–and she alone, who called it. So let her be the one to speak first."

The rats on the wall pointed their heads from speaker to accused, their whiskers twitching wildly as they communicated silently with one another, commenting on the proceedings.

"You don't fool anyone, Kha'i," said Dhama, folding his arms across his chest. "We all know it is you who has orchestrated this. Therefore, *you* called this meeting, in fact. So *you* speak, and be quick about it."

Jasmine furrowed her brow in confusion. The wizened old chuwa knew damn well it was she who insisted on the meeting, arguing against his counsel. What was he playing at, then?

"What do you mean by that?" she said to him.

"Gaoler!" cried The Host, her voice echoing out of the chamber and into the caverns.

From another corridor, opposite to her, came the sound of chains rattling. They didn't sound large enough to be the ones collared to the rat-monster, so she held her breath hoping it was her Raza. Perhaps Kha'i anticipated her tactics already?

What emerged instead was another chuwa, this one sporting deep scars on his cranium and large hoops piercing his nose and exposed genitals. He led a bedraggled man in wrist-cuffs, but he was too short to be Raza. When the Gaoler shoved the man to the centre of the room, the light of the torches illuminated the man's face.

"Imran!"

Jasmine almost ran to him, but stayed herself. She hadn't been expecting to see her rickshaw-wallah here, and though she wanted to release him from their captivity, she had to stay the course and wait for them to reveal where her husband was held. Then she would act.

Imran kept his head down, as though utterly defeated. She hoped they hadn't been too brutal on him.

"Your wayward servant," Kha'i sneered.

"He's not my servant," Jasmine protested. "He's

my friend."

A chuckle escaped Kha'i. "Do not presume it was you to whom I was addressing."

The rat-man turned to face a corridor entrance to her far right, and she finally saw that there was yet another vested party present. Leaning nonchalantly in the opening was Dhōkhā, his painted gypsies corralled behind him.

"It seems he has betrayed you, just as you betrayed us," said Kha'i contemptuously.

At a nod from the Jamallan leader, the Gaoler unlocked Imran's cuffs. The rickshaw-wallah made a dash for the closest unmanned corridor, but the Gaoler had lightning reflexes, his powerful arm shooting out and taking hold of Imran by the neck, lifting the man off the floor. The creature flung Imran across the room like a ragdoll. Jasmine winced as the poor rickshaw-wallah landed hard against the stone floor, rolling to the feet of the gypsies.

Dhōkhā scowled down at the man.

"You goat, Imran. You betrayed me? Just to protect this white woman?"

Another of the gypsies stepped forward.

"You like looking at her with those eyes that *we* gave to you? She'll never love you back, you know."

With a tilt of Dhōkhā's head, the rest of his troupe stooped to clutch at the rickshaw-wallah.

"Take back that which we gave to him," ordered Dhōkhā.

A dagger was produced as Imran was held tight. One of the gypsies held his eyelids open.

"No!" yelled Jasmine, moving to intervene.

Kha'i glided across the floor, hissing at her.

"This is not your business," he snarled, baring his

filed teeth.

She saw Dhama and the Mohallans step forward, ready to advance should Kha'i attack her. So there really was a covenant in place, she realised. In having been turned by the Arms Bearer, it made her Mohallan, and the treaty said Kha'i and his tribe couldn't touch her. But should they, then the Mohallans had rights to defend her. But of Imran, there was nothing she could do. He was human, and he'd made his own deals with these people, which he'd evidently reneged on. This was the price he had to pay.

The rickshaw-wallah screamed as the blade-bearer got to work, scooping the gifted eyeballs from Imran's head. The deed done, Imran lay upon the stone floor weeping softly, blood smeared across his face. Dhōkhā held the scuppered eyeballs in the flat of his palm for all to see, before rolling them inside a leather pouch strapped to his waist.

"You monsters," growled Jasmine, regarding the gypsies with disgust.

"So, *goree*, what is it you are here to discuss?" said Kha'i smugly. "Or is it to be more death?"

Ignoring the chuckling of the Jamallan chuwa, Jasmine gathered her wits to speak.

"I just want my husband," she said. "Plain and simple."

"Very direct," grinned Kha'i.

"Why wouldn't I be?" Jasmine shot back. "You took him. I was there."

Kha'i looked around at his tribe, amused by Jasmine's pluck.

"He was marked, so he belongs to us," he said, eyes shimmering with barely-concealed anticipation.

"I assume you've a bargain to make?"

Dhama stared hard at her, his eyes pleading with her to reconsider. He looked stricken.

"I do," she boldly announced, stepping forward to stand by the dais in the centre of the room. "I'll trade places with my husband, Raza. Free him, and you can have me."

There were gasps and whispers amongst the chuwa, on both sides.

"Why this, Jasmine?" beseeched Dhama. "They have planned this from the beginning. It's what they want."

She surveyed the chamber, the Jamallans and Mohallans standing off against one another, the gypsies standing territorially over a prostrate Imran, the congregation of rats lining the walls. At the monkey she paused, staring at it as if to impart some mental message. The monkey forsook its perch amongst the rats, scrambling down the wall and into the corridor from whence it first came.

"It's the only way, that's why," snapped Jasmine. "You said so yourself, just now. They planned it. I came to you for help, old man, and you left me hanging."

Kha'i broke into a sharp-toothed grin.

"For shame, Dhama," he tutted, shaking his head.

"You are making a mistake, Jasmine," said Dhama, ignoring his foe. "There will be terrible consequences for us all."

"I've already paid my price," she retorted, nearly laughing. "How about it, Kha'i?"

The rat-man smiled appreciably at Jasmine's valour. He arched a thin brow.

"The best laid schemes of mice and men have

come to fruition," he said.

Behind him, his tribe broke into applause, whistling and cheering. It unsettled Jasmine, but as she had insisted, she'd been left no choice.

"There's one more," she said when the celebrations had waned enough for her to be heard.

Kha'i spun around.

"One more what?"

She nodded to where Imran lay on the floor. "Release him, too. Release him from his bonds to any of you."

Her effrontery tickled the rat-man, making him chuckle aloud. The gypsies laughed along with him, though Jasmine's keen sense of supernatural perceptions detected a tremor of unease in them. They might have been ingrained within the politics of the supernatural world, but Dhōkhā and his squad knew when they were out of their depth.

"You think your life is worth two?" wheezed the rat-man.

Jasmine didn't move a muscle; she simply stared at him.

"Yes."

The chuwa with the vitiligo – Pirak, Kha'i had called him – laughed out loud. There was clearly no love lost between him and his leader. As the congregation all turned their faces to Kha'i his mirth evaporated, replaced by a smouldering resentment. His lip curled and a low snarl escaped his throat. As quickly as his mood had changed, it shifted again. He feigned a lackadaisical attitude, looking to the gypsies for their decision. Imran was, after all, under their control.

"Steal the goose, and give the giblets in alms,"

Kha'i said cryptically.

Dhōkhā shrugged.

"Fine, what do we care?" he said. "There are many desperate rickshaw-wallahs ready to indulge our bidding."

The gypsy kicked Imran in the ribs, sending the poor man rolling across the floor to Jasmine's feet. She helped him stand, feeling sympathy for his suffering despite spying on her at the behest of the gypsies. He was a poor man, with good intentions, and he'd simply been caught up in the wrong crowd. She turned him until he faced the cave that led back to Shah Jamal, and to freedom.

"Go straight, and don't stop until you are in the arms of humans again," she whispered.

Reluctantly he staggered forward, scuffing his feet along the floor to feel for hazards.

"Stay the course, rickshaw-wallah," shouted Kha'i devilishly, "lest you wander into the arms of our precious beast guarding the cells."

A chorus of lynch-mob laughter from the Jamallan tribe rose up at their leader's taunts.

Jasmine glowered at them, grinding her teeth.

"That's one part of the deal done," she reminded them.

"Enough of your nonsense, Kha'i," snapped Dhama impatiently. "Just give the girl what she came for."

"Fine, it's done," sneered Kha'i. "You belong to us now, hair-like-the-sun."

Jasmine was unfazed by his buoyancy.

"And Raza? You'll release him now?"

Dhama shuffled forward, careful not to step on the channels carved into the floor.

"We will take him," he declared. "If you agree, Jasmine, I promise none will touch your husband for the remainder of his time in Pakistan. He will have our protection."

Her nostrils flared as she inhaled deeply and let it out in a protracted exhale. Conflicting emotions played across Jasmine's face, but if anything, she mostly felt relief and gratitude. She hadn't known how events might unfold, and what assurances she might wrangle for Raza upon his release, but this offer was above and beyond her expectations.

She nodded at the wizened Mohallan, on the verge of tears.

"I want to see you give my husband to them," she told Kha'i. "I need to see it. Do it, or I'll ruin your deal."

Kha'i considered her request, stroking the tuft of ebon hair on his chin.

"We'll bring him blindfolded, and Dhama can take him," he said. "After that, no more demands. But remember this: if you so much as utter one word to him, we cut his throat open on the spot. He is still ours until in *their* custody."

Jasmine swallowed. It wasn't much of a deal if she couldn't be reunited with her lover, if only for a moment.

"And should you think to break this condition after he is with the Mohallans," cautioned Kha'i, "just keep in mind that by then *you* are in *my* custody."

Jasmine's heart filled with pure hatred for the Jamallan, her breathing laboured as she stared at him soundlessly. She fought the bestial urge to attack him, an urge she'd not have had back when she was entirely human. These were new responses within her that she'd need to learn to manage. She thrust her chin in the air, and the rat-man took it as her concession.

Kha'i turned to the Gaoler and gave the chuwa a curt nod.

"Bring the human," Kha'i said.

Jasmine was relieved to hear that Raza had not been turned. It was all she could hope for, and it made her heart ache to know her darling husband had been spared her fate.

The Gaoler sang softly to himself as he lumbered away into the darkness of a passage.

CHAPTER 24

He was there, on the other side of the Elucidation Chamber, standing betwixt the parted Jamallans, a blindfold over his eyes and cuffs on his wrists: her Raza.

Jasmine was about to call out to him, to reassure her husband that she was here and all would be okay, but a warning glance from Kha'i reminded her of the deal they'd made, and she held her tongue. As the Gaoler tugged Raza across the room, Jasmine studied her husband head to toe. He was malnourished: his lips were chapped and his cheeks hollow, his wrists grazed where the cuffs had rubbed the skin raw.

Raza stumbled disorientated as he was led across the room, slightly hunched as though his legs ached. Jasmine figured the Jamallans must have had him shackled in a small cell for days. She hated them even more for it.

The compulsion to call his name was overwhelming, and fighting it broke her heart. Tears streamed down her face, and her body shook. She needed to hold him, to hear him speak, to know he was not alone. That she was right here. But she'd made a promise and the Machiavellian glint in Kha'i's eyes as he sadistically watched her suffer told her it would be a fatal mistake for either of them.

When a sob escaped her, resounding against the rock walls of the Elucidation Chamber, Raza stopped and cocked his head, listening intently.

Kha'i lips peeled back slowly, revealing the rows of sharpened fangs. Jasmine held her hands over her mouth, slowly shaking her head at the Jamallan.

"Come, boy," said Dhama, worriedly looking to Jasmine.

She knew he hoped to nullify any trouble her outburst might cause. The Gaoler shoved Raza toward the Mohallan, and Dhama's arms wrapped around him as he fell, catching him and standing him upright.

Grief filled Jasmine like a wellspring, disorientating her. Her vision swam as Dhama guided her blindfolded husband from the chamber towards the outside world, his tribe of Mohallan chuwa following solemnly behind. Velli was the last to depart, and she stood at the entrance to the cavern, looking sorrowfully at Jasmine.

Kha'i gave a signal with his fingers in the air, and Pirak – the chuwa with the vitiligo – marched forward to clasp an iron collar around Jasmine's neck, padlocking it on either side. From it hung a heavy chain, which the Gaoler held in his meaty fists. Pirak raised his brows at Jasmine before he retreated to a spot beside the wall.

Velli lifted her hand, placing it over her heart. Jasmine recognised the gesture, and broke into tears as the rat-woman vanished into the darkness of the corridor.

The time for tears was over, decided Jasmine, wiping them on her sleeve. She gave the collar a cursory tug, to test its locks.

"A temporary device," Kha'i chuckled, running his fingers along the outline of the fish-like symbol painted atop the dais. "Much stronger bonds await you, dear."

"You'll find me harder to break than my husband," snarled Jasmine.

Kha'i laughed.

"I'm counting on it, *Mai-m-Mîn*," he said.

A whip, studded along its length with silver ball bearings, was placed in his waiting hand. He folded the whip in half and snapped it threateningly, with a vicious leer.

CHAPTER 25

In the pre-dawn light, Raza was dumped at the doorstep of his grandmother's home by three mysterious figures wearing robes. The blindfold had slipped during the sojourn home and he'd seen his captors sitting in eerie silence, their faces covered by their hoods. A muezzin's call to prayer from several streets away woke the pigeons roosting on the eaves, their wings slapping loudly as they took to the air and flew away. His wrists were still shackled together by the cuffs he'd worn in his underground cell. His vision had returned sometime during his incarceration, and though he'd been blindfolded since his recovery, he still had caught a glimpse of one of his captors as they'd tied the fabric over his eyes. If he hadn't known any better, he'd have sworn it was a monster, half-human and half-animal.

He could hear the footsteps of his kidnappers retreating, but he counted only a pair of them. That meant a third lingered close by. Hands over his, the cuffs relinquishing their bite on his wrists as they unlatched and fell away. He rubbed at his irritated skin, could feel the abrasions.

Something tickled his cheek, like whiskers, as he heard a voice by his ear inform him of the worse.

"Your wife is dead," the stranger said, and Raza

thought he could detect a note of regret. "Forget her. Go back to your home, across the seas."

The pitter-patter of feet told him the last of his kidnappers was going, so Raza tore at his blindfold and stared after the bastard, catching sight only of the robes it wore. He began to give chase, but his legs buckled beneath him and cramps tore across his midriff. He was severely malnourished, his muscles atrophied from sitting in a cell for however long he'd been there. It had been dark, was all he knew, and the overpowering stench of urine had been a constant companion. It was as though his kidnappers had had no sense of hygiene and went wherever they'd pleased.

Animals, he thought to himself.

They were gone now, the mysterious figures, and he knew they'd have easily outpaced him by now and escaped into Lahore's millions. He glanced over his shoulder at the house, and hoped Jasmine would be inside. She'd be sick with worry, of course, but he was home now, and he'd promise her they'd never return.

Raza hobbled up the steps and tested the front door. It swung open, creaking in the silence of the house.

"Jasmine!"

There was no answer, so he called again, and again. He tried his grandmother, but she, too, didn't answer. With effort he searched the house, calling desperately and hoping just as desperately that his wife and grandmother would heed his call and come to him, comfort and heal him.

But the house was empty.

Inspector Ghumman tapped his pen against his knee in a way that began to really irritate Raza. The police had been in the house for two hours now, combing for evidence that he and Jasmine had simply quarrelled and she'd fled back to Australia. Raza had been incensed by the suggestion, firing back at them about the inadequacies of their profession. It had only strengthened the officers' resolve to find Raza guilty of domestic violence, and thus rest their case. They had one vital clue to support their theory: a hank of Jasmine's hair, found on the floor of the kitchen amongst a litter of broken plates and upended pans. Only Ghumman, in a crisp navy blue suit and shiny grey tie, seemed to have sympathy for Raza's version of events.

"Please forgive the officers, Mr Makhdoom," he said, twitching his nose as though it itched. "They don't have the wherewithal that men of grace such as ourselves possess."

From the outset, the Inspector had been at pains to impress upon Raza the idea that he was of a different breed to his peers. Raza couldn't have given a rat's arse, in fact.

"But it's true," Raza ranted. "Why would I fucking lie about this! I was kidnapped by these bastards! Maybe they have my wife also!"

The officers stared at him until he'd finished, grinning at one another as they continued to search the drawers in the lounge area.

"But a secret cult?" said Ghumman gently.

"Why not?" huffed Raza. "They're all over the bloody place here."

Ghumman indulged Raza a little smile of acknowledgement at the accusation.

"But supernatural cults?" he persisted.

Raza rested his head in his hands, fighting the feeling of sickness washing over him. He'd lost a lot of weight, and felt lightheaded after his ordeal. The incredulity of the lawmen wasn't helping. Inspector Ghumman snapped at the officers, directing them to continue their shameful search elsewhere on the premises. When it was only the two of them, Ghumman reached out and patted Raza's arm.

"You've been through a lot, I can see," he said. "It has taken a toll on you. The mind can play tricks when that happens."

Raza raised his head, eyes red from the tears he'd shed earlier.

"Look, Inspector, I know it's hard to believe. But there really are monsters out there..."

Ghumman continued to regard Raza with a look of sympathy, pursing his lips patiently as he listened once again to the story of cults and creatures in the streets of Lahore. From the hallway Raza could hear the police officers snorting in derision.

"Fuck it!" he spat.

The ticking of the clock-hands on the wall was the only sound as Raza sat staring at the window, wondering what could have happened to Jasmine. Thoughts tumbled through his mind, scenarios he'd never have wished to imagine, each building in horror upon the last. There was no note, from either Jasmine or the kidnappers. There were only the signs of struggle in the kitchen, and a lock of her hair torn from the roots, presumably during the melee. And where was Malika in all of this? Did they take her, too?

"Can you find her, Inspector?" he asked so quietly Ghumman almost missed it.

The Inspector let the gravity of the question have its due time, before answering with earnest.

"I'll be frank with you," he started. "You know, this is Pakistan. I think you know it's not always the most lawful place. I don't think this investigation will end happily. I think you know this, too."

Raza stared at the floor, and slowly closed his eyes.

"We will look, Mr Makhdoom. I guarantee you. We will do our best. And I'm sure there will be a thorough investigation from the Australian authorities, too. But I won't bullshit you, Raza."

The Inspector seemed a little too impressed by his own use of an Australian idiom, thought Raza, but he appreciated the effort all the same, even if he couldn't show it. Ghumman stood, patting Raza's shoulder.

"I've noted everything here, and have all that I need," he said, his soft fingers respectfully folding the ziplock evidence bag containing Jasmine's hair. "I'll leave an officer outside, if you want?"

Raza shook his head. He knew in his heart that the kidnappers had taken all they would from this house. If they'd wanted Raza still, he'd currently be shackled to a dank prison stinking of urine. He was no longer part of the equation, he understood.

"I'll be back tomorrow," Ghumman promised. "We'll go over it some more. Maybe you could take me to where you had these problems with the mafia's man, behind Badshahi. Until then, try and rest."

Ghumman wandered to the door, waiting as the police officers shuffled out one by one. As he was about to exit, he paused, looking back over his shoulder.

"Oh, and Raza..."

Raza glanced up from his meditation.

"No more talk of monsters," the Inspector advised. "It doesn't look good, you know?"

The Inspector tapped the side of his skull, and Raza inferred his meaning. This was now a house of intrigue, and the neighbours would be watching his every move. But that was a good thing, thought Raza. The home would have around-the-clock security monitoring, whether it was the intention or not.

Inspector Ghumman admired the bright light of day, and cheerily stepped over the threshold, gently closing the door behind him, plunging Raza into darkness and deep thought.

Out on the street a small girl in rags ran up to the Inspector, holding her grubby little hand out as if for alms. Ghumman wrinkled his nose up at the smell of the girl. Clearly another gutter-rat sleeping in trash piles. Ghumman reached into his jacket, producing the ziplock bag of hair. He held it up to the sky, marvelling at how the blonde tresses caught the brilliance of the sun. He'd never touched such yellow hair before, and had to admit it held a certain power over him. It was with reluctance he handed it to the little girl begging before him.

As if she, too, were as entranced by the contents of the bag, the girl held it against the sun, staring in wide-eyed wonder. A sharp whistle from the lowered window of the car down the street broke her somnambulism, and she sprinted in its direction, the bag waving around in her hand as though it now held little value. The girl handed it through the window, receiving a five-hundred rupee note in exchange, which she slipped into her shirt as she darted across the street and into a laneway, out of sight.

The car rolled slowly down the street, tyres crunching on gravel and dry donkey dung, until it came abreast of the Inspector.

Peering out was the head honcho of the Lakar Baga Badmash – just one of many mafia corporations operating in Lahore – Lakar Baga himself, his heavy jowls resting over the lapels of his luxurious *kameez*. With a shudder, Ghumman realised one of those cursed chuwa sat beside the mafia boss, staring out at him with those big, black eyes in which Ghumman could never discern a trace of thought or emotion. He hated conversing with those creatures at the best of times, let alone during a high-profile investigation such as this. Aru-Min was the chuwa's name, if he recalled correctly. He remembered because it was the one who liked to adorn itself with an obscene amount of bejewelled necklaces and gold bracelets, some throwback to priesthood in the Harappan age, Ghumman had once heard.

"You've done well, Inspector," said Lakar Baga, opening the bag and rubbing the strands of hair between his fingers.

"And the human?" rasped the rat-man.

Ghumman addressed the mafia boss, unable to contend with the chuwa's presence.

"Mr Makhdoom will be arrested tomorrow," he confided. "Suspected murder of his wife and grandmother."

The mafia boss strained his fat head in the creature's direction, and Aru-Min nodded almost imperceptibly, never taking his midnight eyes from the Inspector. Lakar Baga grinned hungrily as he passed the ziplock bag of hair back to the Inspector, whose eagle eyes noticed the mafia boss had plucked a few strands free to keep for himself.

Ghumman wiped at the sweat on his brow, blaming the heat of the day for it, though the smirk on Lakar Baga's chubby lips told him the *goonda* knew it was a knot of fear developing in his gut. Ghumman couldn't help it; the rat-man's scrutiny was unnerving.

The window wound up, to Ghumman's relief, reflecting his own sweaty, pale face back at himself. The vehicle drove off, spinning its back tyres on the gravel to cloud the Inspector in dust. Ghumman didn't care, so long as his audience with the mafia, and more importantly, the chuwa, was over for another day. He'd count the days until he'd have to interact with either again.

Pocketing the evidence bag, he glanced back up at the Makhdoom's house, ignoring the inquisitiveness of the neighbours. The sound of screaming came from inside, as the young man released his grief and fury. He'd bring the boy a box of *gulab jamun* tomorrow, something sweet to ease the sense of shock, just before he had him dragged down to the station and questioned rigorously.

Ghumman walked over to where the mini-van of police officers waited, singing brusquely to the love ballads blaring from the radio. After their boorish performance in the house, he wondered how much they really knew of love. The engine rumbled to life, drowning out the hoarse screaming coming from the house, and the driver eased the van down the street and into the slipstream of Lahore's insane traffic.

EPILOGUE

The party at Shah Jamal was in full swing, Sufi's twirling feverishly on the spot in the middle of a drunken crowd of young men, while the *dholis* at their backs beat a furious tempest upon the skins. It was a scene repeated a few nights of every week, especially on Thursdays for some reason. Jasmine didn't understand why, and no-one had yet bothered explaining it to her.

She sat high in the branches of the ficus tree, overlooking proceedings, deriving a simple pleasure from the rhythmic thump of the drums. Once upon a time, in a faraway land, she might have been perched on a stool with friends at a nightclub, the bass of a sound-system vibrating in her skull as she watched a dance-floor of revellers twist and flail their arms. The Jamallans had allowed her this one reprieve from their suffocating life in the urine-drenched caverns beneath the tombs, where Kha'i plotted, waiting patiently for the event he claimed would change everything.

Personally, Jasmine thought the rat-faced bastard was touched alright; touched in the head. She hadn't had much personal contact with madness in her life, but she supposed Kha'i's obsession with dominating the city was in tune with that paradigm.

And he was cruel, too. Jasmine had already

suffered broken bones and beatings for her insolence. She healed quickly, thankfully, but her pride took the greater bruising in that respect: she still seethed at the memory of his blows.

Several weeks had passed since the fateful day she'd given herself to the Jamallan chuwa in exchange for her husband's life, and though a day didn't pass where she wasn't grateful for his release, she fretted nonetheless. She was denied access to phones and internet here, so there was no way to contact her family in Australia and learn if Raza had made it home safely. To know if Dhama had kept his word, and ferried her husband to safety. It was the only thing bonding Jasmine to her side of the deal: while Raza was still within reach of Kha'i and his rats, she must remain under his dominion, or risk her husband's life. To abscond now would be to have fought for naught.

A movement in the braches alerted her to the presence of an intruder. Her chuwa eyes pierced the darkness, but nobody was there. If another chuwa had climbed to her, she'd smell them immediately. And if any of the drug or alcohol fuelled humans below had attempted, she'd have heard them on their first footing within the myriad branches.

She reached out her keen olfactory senses, detecting a musty odour that was mostly animal. She sniffed again. It was monkey she could smell.

A bushel of leaves was pushed aside and a small monkey with golden eyes carefully crept into view, keeping its distance from her. It perused the dancing below, watching her from its periphery. When she draped a hand across her knee, the monkey flinched, staring at her with wide eyes and bared teeth as though it expected her to pounce upon it. She swung her leg playfully from her perch, and the monkey relaxed.

"The rest of you can come out," she drawled.

Then the canopy of the great tree shook as a dozen monkeys descended through the branches, coalescing with the first until he sat there, the strange man with the big teeth and the golden eyes: Iqbal.

He possessed the same furtive anxiety as the monkey, unable to maintain eye-contact for long. The party below distracted him, and Jasmine supposed he'd never partaken in such activities in his life.

"What do you want?" she said.

"I have news," he said meekly.

She perked up, making him uneasy. She thought

perhaps he'd come to gloat, or even apologise. But his words set aflame a combustion inside her, and her sanity would depend on the direction the Monkey-Man's news might take. Her pulse quickened, blood rushing through her temples.

Iqbal swallowed, cleared his throat. "They put him in the gaol."

She didn't need to ask who. Either who was in the gaol, or who put him there. Jasmine knew straight away: for whatever reason, Raza had been arrested and imprisoned in Pakistan.

Kha'i had won, finally. With Raza still on the continent and possibly available to Kha'i's circle of influence, Jasmine had no choice but to remain a captive of the Jamallan sect of chuwa. Their covenant would remain intact, and whatever insidious ambition Kha'i held for her, it would be enacted.

"Then it's all over," she whispered, staring down at the Sufi's spinning wildly.

They looked free, of spirit and mind and soul. She'd give anything to drop from the branches in their midst, landing on her clawed hands and feet, and take up their dance, twirling until all reason and ego had spun from her, all pain and sorrow had sweated from her pores.

"There's another way," the Monkey-Man said quietly.

She looked him square in the eyes, and this time he didn't flinch or look away. Instead, he smiled at her, his crooked teeth like a broken picket fence.

"Show me," said Jasmine.